Thespian Playworks 2015

Escalator
by Tanner Heath

Atlas's Equal
by Austin Hughes

The Okay Kids
by Hunter McKenzie

It's Gonna Rain
by Matthew Waterman

A SAMUEL FRENCH ACTING EDITION

SAMUEL FRENCH

FOUNDED 1830

SAMUELFRENCH.COM
SAMUELFRENCH-LONDON.CO.UK

FOR PRODUCTION ENQUIRIES

UNITED STATES AND CANADA
Info@SamuelFrench.com
1-866-598-8449

UNITED KINGDOM AND EUROPE
Plays@SamuelFrench-London.co.uk
020-7255-4302

Each title is subject to availability from Samuel French, depending upon country of performance. Please be aware that *THESPIAN PLAYWORKS 2015* may not be licensed by Samuel French in your territory. Professional and amateur producers should contact the nearest Samuel French office or licensing partner to verify availability.

FOREWORD

A play is not a weather report. It's *supposed* to be ambiguous.

The 2015 Thespian Playworks finalists all have a gift for what might be called dramatic meteorology: reading the signs; observing established patterns of human behavior; considering new variables, both known and unknown, and finally suggesting—without actually predicting—how a particular emotional storm system might play out.

The four teenaged writers spent a week in June, at the Thespian Festival in Lincoln, Nebraska, practicing this imprecise art with teams of professional directors and dramaturgs, student actors, and enthusiastic audiences. They wrestled with a lot of questions while putting their subtle stories in motion: Whose play is it? What do these characters really want, and why? Do they get it? How and when do we know? What comes next?

Some of those answers are still taking shape for Tanner Heath, of Rutland (Vermont) High School, who wrote *Escalator*; Austin Hughes, a graduate of James W. Martin High School in Arlington, Texas, now at the University of Iowa (*Atlas's Equal*); Hunter McKenzie, a graduate of Winnacunnet High School in Hampton, New Hampshire, now at Columbia College in Chicago (*The Okay Kids*); and Bloomington (Indiana) High School North graduate Matthew Waterman (*It's Gonna Rain*), who's now at Indiana University.

"Playworks made me feel like I am a playwright," Matthew Waterman recently told us via email. "Before Playworks, I thought my script was possibly really good or possibly really bad. Now I'm fairly certain that it's fairly good, but not great. However, I definitely think it got better throughout the week. After the Playworks experience, I am more certain that I will continue to write and submit scripts, and that I will pursue playwriting (or film and TV writing) as part of my career."

We like that forecast. And we see another favorable sign in this handsome acting edition of the four finalist scripts—an annual Playworks tradition thanks to our friends at Samuel French, Inc., a longtime sponsor of the program. Their support, along with your interest in the creative findings of these young dramatists/social climatologists, suggests bright days ahead for the American theatre.

— Julie York Coppens
Senior Associate Editor, Dramatics Magazine

CONTENTS

Escalator

by
Tanner Heath

ESCALATOR was presented in a staged reading as part of the Thespian Playworks program at the 2015 Thespian Festival on June 26. William Myatt was Director, Steve Gregg served as Dramaturg, and Maura Wetzel served as Stage Manager. The cast was as follows:

CHARACTER 1 . . . . .Noelle Soucek

CHARACTER 2 . . . . Caleb Duane

CHARACTER 3 . . . . .Raven McGowan

CHARACTER 4 . . . . .Angel Martinez

CHARACTER 5 . . . . .Megan Flanagan

CHARACTER 6 . . . . Noah Loux

CHARACTER 7 . . . . Lucky Vemuri

ABOUT THE PLAYWRIGHT

Tanner Heath wrote *Escalator* during his junior year at Rutland High School in Rutland, Vermont. Several of his ten-minute plays have been selected and performed at the Weston Playhouse, and *Escalator* was his first one-act play. He would like to thank his Director Cathy Archer for encouraging him to step outside his comfort zone and write. He would also like to thank his whole family for supporting him and attending his shows regardless of the travel distance. He gives one last thank-you to Playworks for giving such an amazing, life-changing opportunity to high school students. He plans on writing more in the future because of this experience.

CHARACTERS

CHARACTER 1 – Teenage girl

CHARACTER 2 – Teenage boy

CHARACTER 3 – Young girl

CHARACTER 4 – Man in his mid-thirties

CHARACTER 5 – Woman in her twenties

CHARACTER 6 – Man in his twenties

CHARACTER 7 – Woman in her early forties

SETTING

A busy mall with an escalator at the center.

(Lights up on four boxes center stage. From stage right to stage left, they are next to each other from shortest to tallest. Characters walk on in a row from stage right. They step onto the stage in unison, and proceed up the boxes in synchronization, until **CHARACTER 1** *is at the top,* **CHARACTER 2** *is on the second box,* **CHARACTER 3** *and* **CHARACTER 4** *are on the third box,* **CHARACTER 5** *is on the lowest box, and* **CHARACTER 6** *is on the floor. When all characters are in place there is a loud screech followed by a bang, and they all lurch forward suddenly.)*

CHARACTER 1. What happened?

CHARACTER 2. I don't know…

CHARACTER 3. Is this what the end of the world feels like? I don't want to die!

CHARACTER 4. *(Taking out his earbuds.)* There must be a logical explanation… Right?

CHARACTER 5. *(Looking up from the book she was reading on her tablet.)* Oh of course this would happen to me!

CHARACTER 1. Hold on, I'll Google it. *(She looks at her iPhone for a few seconds and types frantically. After a few seconds she gives a sigh of defeat.)* It's no use. This mall doesn't have any service!

CHARACTER 4. I think I read something about that! The article it was mentioned in said something like "metal support beams can bounce the signal back at the phone and create a sort of dead zone."

CHARACTER 2. What does that even mean?

CHARACTER 4. It means your phone won't work here.

CHARACTER 3. Great! We might be stuck here for hours, even days! I don't want to go like this.

CHARACTER 6. What is the holdup? I have places to be.

CHARACTER 5. Please calm down. I have too much on my plate to worry about this.

CHARACTER 4. If you must know, the escalator has stopped. No one here is going anywhere soon.

CHARACTER 3. Maybe someone can see what's going on at the top.

CHARACTER 1. I can't see past all of the other people.

CHARACTER 6. I'll go get help! But… I can't get off, this is the up escalator.

CHARACTER 2. So what do we do now? Sit here and count dust bunnies?

CHARACTER 4. This seems like the perfect time to get to know each other!

CHARACTER 2. I could care less who you are.

CHARACTER 1. What would getting to know any of you do for me?

CHARACTER 5. We might be able to figure out strengths and weaknesses.

CHARACTER 2. I don't see how any of this will help. Why don't we just sit and wait until someone comes and gets us down.

CHARACTER 4. That could take days, even weeks! We don't have that long. Now is the time for action!

CHARACTER 3. Weeks? We might be up here for weeks! We're doomed!

CHARACTER 2. Way to stay positive.

CHARACTER 1. Taking shots at a little girl. How macho.

CHARACTER 2. I'm just saying that she's not helping at all.

CHARACTER 5. Well she's trying the best she can. It's obviously very scary for her.

CHARACTER 2. What about the rest of us?

CHARACTER 5. What about us?

CHARACTER 2. We are all up here, in the same situation.

CHARACTER 4. Well you aren't as young as she is.

CHARACTER 1. Though you act as if you are.

CHARACTER 2. What did you say?

CHARACTER 1. I certainly did not say anything at all about your childish behavior.

CHARACTER 2. I'm sorry that I have other things to do besides stand here all day stuck with this lot.

CHARACTER 6. Do you think that we want to be here?

CHARACTER 2. No one seems to be taking any positive action.

CHARACTER 5. Well we were trying to assess the situation. But you had to keep going on.

CHARACTER 4. Then let us return to the situation. What should be our first step? Any suggestions?

CHARACTER 1. I will call for help!

CHARACTER 2. There is still no connection of any sort here. Geez, you have the memory of a goldfish.

CHARACTER 5. There you go with those snide remarks.

CHARACTER 6. Guys. All of us are stuck together on this escalator. Bickering won't help the situation.

CHARACTER 3. Except you're not actually on the escalator.

CHARACTER 6. Speak up, please?

CHARACTER 3. You can walk away, you're not on it yet, trapped without hope like we are. Oh I don't want to die! *(Sits down on box.)*

CHARACTER 4. She's right! You are not standing on the escalator. You can turn around and walk away!

CHARACTER 6. I guess I'm not really on the escalator.

CHARACTER 1. Then get going. My friends are expecting me.

        (CHARACTER 6 *leaves.)*

CHARACTER 2. Our only hope of survival is in that man… We might as well give up now.

CHARACTER 1. Guys, I'll text my friend and have her send help! *(Looks at her phone then sighs.)* Oh, I forgot. No service.

CHARACTER 2. This sucks.

CHARACTER 5. So what is the plan now?

CHARACTER 4. I remember watching a survival show once, and they said that when you are in a dangerous situation ration your food so that it will last as long as possible.

CHARACTER 3. Does anyone have food?

CHARACTER 1. I have some gum. But you can't swallow it. Cause then it will be stuck in you for years… But then again, our stomachs would be filled.

CHARACTER 4. That's not a real thing. It's just something you say to your kids so that they don't swallow gum and choke.

CHARACTER 1. Oh… Well I'm supposed to be meeting my friends in the food court soon, so when I don't show up they might come looking for me.

CHARACTER 2. What are the odds that your "friends" will? They might just think you stood them up.

CHARACTER 1. What is that supposed to mean?

CHARACTER 2. How close are you to these people?

CHARACTER 1. I text them all the time. And follow them on Twitter and Instagram.

CHARACTER 2. Exactly. You didn't mention talking to them, just using your phone to connect to their phone. Sounds like a crappy friendship to me.

CHARACTER 1. I don't see any of your friends coming to help us out.

CHARACTER 2. I don't see your friends either. At least when I talk to my friends it's face-to-face.

CHARACTER 5. Some of us have bigger problems than worrying about our friends.

CHARACTER 4. We need to stop turning on ourselves. If we are going to be up here together we at least have to tolerate each other.

CHARACTER 2. Or we could just give up. That is a lot easier.

CHARACTER 5. This can't be it. I can't leave things how I did.

CHARACTER 1. What do you mean by that?

CHARACTER 5. Me and…and my fiancé… We… Things aren't okay.

CHARACTER 4. Just let it out. It's okay.

CHARACTER 2. Cause we care so much.

CHARACTER 5. *(Almost in tears)* I… I ju…just can't. *(Sits down on box, crying.)*

CHARACTER 3. I want my mom! *(Sits down on box.)*

CHARACTER 2. And just like that, two down. Two to go.

CHARACTER 1. Why don't you just shut up. You're making this a lot worse.

CHARACTER 2. You'll be next, blondie.

CHARACTER 1. Oh, you wanna go? I watched a video on kung fu once. I'll take you down.

CHARACTER 2. Whoa, the five-foot blond girl is going to take me down. Watch out, or your phone might break.

CHARACTER 4. Stop it you two. There's no telling how long we will be stuck here. We need to cooperate.

CHARACTER 1. The only way my phone will break is if I crack it on your thick skull.

CHARACTER 2. I doubt you are strong enough to swing a flyswatter.

CHARACTER 1. You wanna get off this escalator? How about I push you over the side.

CHARACTER 2. I'm hearing threats but I'm not seeing any actions.

CHARACTER 3. Stop it! Stop it stop it stop it!

CHARACTER 2. Look, now you've upset her.

CHARACTER 1. Me? Really? You're the one who started this.

CHARACTER 2. But I'm not threatening you in any way.

CHARACTER 1. Really? 'Cause, "You'll be next, blondie" sounds like a threat and an insult to me.

CHARACTER 5. Quit it you two. Your fight is pointless.

CHARACTER 2. Oh, so now you decide to give input. Just go back to crying.

CHARACTER 5. What did you just say to me?

CHARACTER 2. I'm just saying that you had an emotional breakdown while we were trying to get out of this mess.

CHARACTER 5. Want to know why? Because I'm about to get married to a man, and last night we had a huge fight. But what do you care about my petty problems.

CHARACTER 2. Well, I didn't know…

CHARACTER 5. Exactly. You didn't know but you were awfully quick to assume that your problems were the biggest in the world.

CHARACTER 1. I doubt he's even kissed a girl. He wouldn't know what relationships are like.

CHARACTER 2. You're one to talk. You just stare blankly at that phone of yours all day.

CHARACTER 1. I am a social butterfly that has to maintain my many connections.

CHARACTER 2. I bet that you haven't talked to half of your "friends" on Facebook in years, let alone seen them.

CHARACTER 1. Sure I have. Everyone updates their profile picture at least once a month.

CHARACTER 2. People around you constantly change but you can't see that in a picture.

CHARACTER 4. In case you have forgotten, we are all stuck together. Fighting will get us nowhere.

CHARACTER 6. *(Returning to his spot on stage from off right, carrying a shoe.)* Guys! Hey guys! I've figured out the problem. Some kid got their shoe stu…

> *(Cut off as* **CHARACTER 7** *walks on from off right and shoves him, causing him to drop the shoe.)*

CHARACTER 7. *(Talking to herself as she walks on, holding makeup compact with a flip-up mirror.)* Oh dear, my lipstick is smudged. The nerve of some people, running into me.

CHARACTER 6. Um… Excuse you ma'am.

CHARACTER 7. Oh, you're excused. *(Again, to herself.)* How dare he talk to me. Filthy peasant. *(She proceeds to walk slowly up the steps, gently pushing people out of the way.)* Why are people in my way? I have places to be.

(She stops on the third step up when **CHARACTER 1** *blocks her.)* Who does she think she is? *(To* **CHARACTER 1.***)* Stand aside.

CHARACTER 1. Who do you think you are?

CHARACTER 7. Who I am is none of your business. My social class is superior to yours.

CHARACTER 1. What did you just say to me?

CHARACTER 7. I was simply pointing out that you have a distinct lack of respect for your superiors. Now remove yourself from my path.

CHARACTER 1. You better keep quiet.

CHARACTER 7. *(To herself.)* She continues to defy my request to move. Teenagers these days.

CHARACTER 1. Oh, you're in for it. Hold my phone! *(Gives phone to* **CHARACTER 2.***)*

CHARACTER 4. Hey, you two! You have bigger issues than each other!

CHARACTER 7. *(To herself.)* What does that fool mean? Maybe he is just a bumbling hobo. Look at the rags he is wearing.

CHARACTER 2. I don't know how you haven't noticed yet.

CHARACTER 7. *(To herself.)* The baboon talks, too!

CHARACTER 2. Hey, wake up lady! This escalator is stopped. We're trapped. And if you took two seconds to look beyond your ego at the world around you, you would realize you walked right into it.

CHARACTER 7. *(Going pale.)* Oh dear.

CHARACTER 1. You're looking a little…ghostly.

CHARACTER 3. Boo!

(CHARACTER 7 emits a sigh so exaggerated it almost causes her to fall off the box. She barely catches herself.)

CHARACTER 4. As funny as that was, a death would make this situation much more complex.

CHARACTER 7. Stay away from me, filthy peasants. I will not stand to be around in this freak show any more. Winston! Winston come and fetch me! *(After a long pause.)* Oh, there you are, Winston! I need you to come and get me out of here.

CHARACTER 6. Is she talking to me?

CHARACTER 7. Of course, Winston.

CHARACTER 6. Um… I'm not Winston.

CHARACTER 7. Ha ha ha. Very funny, Winston. Now get me off this death trap.

CHARACTER 5. Could you please not be so full of yourself?

CHARACTER 7. Winston, hurry up. The giraffe has started talking to me.

CHARACTER 5. Giraffe? Really? That's the best you could do?

CHARACTER 7. Why don't you take your boogery drooling child and leave my presence.

CHARACTER 3. I… I don't… H-have a mother. *(Sits down on escalator.)*

CHARACTER 7. Oh, an orphan? Don't touch me. I can't believe I'm sharing the same escalator as an orphan.

CHARACTER 2. You have ten seconds to find a way out of here before I strangle you myself.

CHARACTER 7. Winston! Hurry up! I can feel the hostility here.

CHARACTER 6. For the last time, I'm not Winston!

CHARACTER 4. Why don't you aim for that fountain down there.

CHARACTER 7. Silly little peasant. Do you really expect me to jump into that fountain?

CHARACTER 4. Here's a tip, spread yourself out. The more of your surface that hits the water, the more water there is to stop you from hitting the bottom.

CHARACTER 7. You can't expect me to ju…

> (**CHARACTER 1** *pushes* **CHARACTER 7** *off the boxes toward the back of the stage. A long scream is heard from* **CHARACTER 7**, *followed by a splash.*)

CHARACTER 1. Oh I need to tweet about this. Wait, where's my phone?

CHARACTER 2. You gave it to me.

CHARACTER 1. Give it.

CHARACTER 4. You've been without your phone for five whole minutes. You set it aside and accomplished something. Guys, do you realize that is the first time we have all been on the same side!

CHARACTER 6. Well now that that whole fiasco is settled, how are we going to get you all off?

CHARACTER 5. Did any of you hear what she just said?

CHARACTER 1. Which part? The part about this kid being a "baboon"?

CHARACTER 5. No not that lady. The little girl.

CHARACTER 4. She said something about being an orphan.

CHARACTER 5. Yes she did.

CHARACTER 2. So…

CHARACTER 5. That could very well be her biggest secret! Go on honey, you can tell us what is wrong.

CHARACTER 3. No.

CHARACTER 2. Anyway… Does anyone have any brilliant ideas to get us down?

CHARACTER 1. Really, how can you be so inconsiderate?

CHARACTER 2. Do I actually care what she says? The fact that she is an orphan does nothing for me.

CHARACTER 1. Are you heartless? This is a little girl we are talking about!

CHARACTER 4. Besides, she may know something that we don't.

CHARACTER 5. And you did say that getting to know each other would help.

CHARACTER 2. Okay, okay. Let's get to know each other then, if you guys really think it will help.

CHARACTER 5. How about we each tell you one of our secrets. I'll start. *(Heavy sigh.)* It's me and my fiancé. We were fighting… Because… Well it was because I've been so stressed lately. The fight was all my fault!

CHARACTER 1. I'm sure it wasn't. He must be stressed too.

CHARACTER 5. Possibly. But I'm afraid of being held down. Marriage is just so scary. There are so many unknowns and anything can go wrong.

CHARACTER 6. I'm not married or anything, but plenty of my friends are getting married. They all seem to be moving on and I'm the only one who is still single. What's worse is they used to drag me to parties, and I hate parties but I would go so people would think that I'm cool. Now I'm alone and socially awkward.

CHARACTER 4. I've been stuck in the same job for years! I want something new and exciting. Something that will make an impact on the world. There are so many different things I could do, but I'm no good at any of them.

CHARACTER 2. What is this, group therapy?

CHARACTER 1. Since you seem so inclined to say things, why don't you go.

CHARACTER 2. You haven't said anything either.

CHARACTER 1. I am afraid of being ostracized. There.

CHARACTER 2. Ostracized is a pretty big word. Are you sure you didn't mean to say that you are afraid of being an ostrich?

CHARACTER 1. Why are you always so negative? It does not help our situation, and even if it makes you feel better, we all feel worse because of it.

CHARACTER 3. *(Quiet and ignored.)* As long as I can remember I have lived in this mall.

CHARACTER 2. Why are you always on your phone? You can't rely on technology as a substitute for everything. Social interactions are one of those things.

CHARACTER 4. Guys, keep your voices down for a second.

CHARACTER 2. Did I miss something important? Are we getting off of this escalator?

CHARACTER 5. No, this little girl said her secret.

CHARACTER 1. What did she say?

CHARACTER 4. That she has lived in this mall all of her life.

CHARACTER 2. Then why did she say that she wanted her mommy earlier?

CHARACTER 4. Don't ask me. Ask her for yourself.

CHARACTER 2. Why did you say you wanted your mommy?

CHARACTER 3. I wanted to sound normal, I guess.

CHARACTER 5. Well nobody is normal. Just look at who you are here with right now.

CHARACTER 1. Speaking of normal, what's your secret? You haven't said yet.

CHARACTER 2. I don't have any secrets. It's one of my best qualities.

CHARACTER 1. Yeah okay.

CHARACTER 2. It's true.

CHARACTER 4. Everyone has a secret, or a fear.

CHARACTER 3. You can tell us.

CHARACTER 2. I just don't! Can we please drop it!

CHARACTER 1. I bet you're afraid of something lame. Like thunder, or the dark! Are you afraid of the dark? That's what it is!

CHARACTER 5. Don't pester him. It's fine.

CHARACTER 2. Ghosts.

CHARACTER 1. What did you say?

CHARACTER 2. I'm afraid of ghosts! Now can we drop it?

CHARACTER 1. You don't need to get so defensive.

CHARACTER 5. Don't you all feel much better now.

CHARACTER 2. No.

CHARACTER 4. Well we definitely know each other better now. Can you really expect to work together with people if you don't know anything about them?

CHARACTER 2. But none of that helps us get off of this escalator!

CHARACTER 1. Sure it does. We are communicating.

CHARACTER 2. Standing here all day holding hands and singing "Kumbaya" doesn't help get us out of here!

CHARACTER 1. Why don't you start yelling again? You might just follow that crazy lady off the escalator.

CHARACTER 6. Hey! We were doing so good getting along.

CHARACTER 5. Unless we are all on the same page, nothing we do will help get us out of here.

CHARACTER 2. Let's stop talking and start acting!

CHARACTER 4. Okay genius, what do you want to do first?

CHARACTER 2. Well… We could… Uh. Did anyone look for emergency kits?

CHARACTER 1. We are on an escalator. Where would they store an emergency kit?

CHARACTER 2. We could make our way to the top.

CHARACTER 5. No one in front of us is moving.

CHARACTER 6. Even if someone made it to the top, the whole thing is roped off for the maintenance guys.

CHARACTER 2. Okay so my ideas are not perfect! But your attitudes aren't going to get us off either.

> *(As "either" is said a loud screech is heard, followed by a bang.)*

CHARACTER 6. Is everyone okay?

CHARACTER 1. It looks like there are workers at the top. And one of them is giving a thumbs up.

CHARACTER 5. We might be getting off!

CHARACTER 2. I think one of them yelled "all clear."

    (Another bang is heard.)

CHARACTER 3. We don't seem to be moving.

CHARACTER 1. Looks like they are shaking their heads. Oh no.

CHARACTER 2. Nice job getting our hopes up.

CHARACTER 1. It wasn't me, it was them.

CHARACTER 4. Even the maintenance guys can't get us off.

CHARACTER 6. They are gesturing something. Are they waving?

CHARACTER 3. Are they leaving us? Is that all there is to it?

CHARACTER 1. No… They're… They're pointing!

CHARACTER 5. At us?

CHARACTER 1. No. At the bottom. I think they want us to walk off.

CHARACTER 4. Can we do that?

CHARACTER 3. No way. This is the up escalator.

CHARACTER 1. It's not like it is moving, though. Let's just do it ourselves.

CHARACTER 5. Worth a shot. *(Looking hesitant, then stepping onto the floor. A sudden fear crosses her face and she flinches before realizing nothing happened.)* I seem okay.

CHARACTER 4. You do seem so.

    (All characters walk off the escalator in reverse of the way they came on, pausing briefly before stepping off and showing fear.)

CHARACTER 2. That seemed too easy.

CHARACTER 1. You're going to complain about being off?

CHARACTER 6. It does seem too easy. But at least you are all safe.

CHARACTER 4. Well, goodbye I guess. Nice meeting you all.

CHARACTER 1. That's it? We survived all that and you are just leaving with a simple goodbye? How about we all exchange numbers or something? I feel like we have grown so close. *(Looks for phone.)* You still have my phone, don't you!

CHARACTER 2. I guess I do. Here you go.

> *(They begin to walk off stage right in a group, while* **CHARACTER 3** *walks off stage left.)*

CHARACTER 1. About that numbers thing. I think we should do a group chat!

CHARACTER 5. You want to call us all up? That will cost a fortune!

CHARACTER 1. No, we can text!

CHARACTER 5. Um… Okay then.

CHARACTER 1. Hold on… We need to take a group selfie to post on Insta.

CHARACTER 5. What exactly is a selfie?

CHARACTER 1. It's a picture that you take of yourself.

CHARACTER 5. Okay. And what is an "Insta"?

CHARACTER 1. That is short for Instagram. *(Long pause).* Instagram! It's like Twitter but with pictures. Geez, what do you do with all of the pictures you take of your Starbucks?

CHARACTER 2. Did any of you see where the little girl went?

CHARACTER 1. Maybe she is a ghost! Are you scared?

> *(There is a pause after the group walks offstage right, then* **CHARACTER 7** *walks out from behind the escalator. She is soaked, holding her head, and looking flustered. As* **CHARACTER 7** *continues with her scene,* **CHARACTER 3** *walks on, goes over to the shoe—she's been missing it all this time—sits down, and puts it on.* **CHARACTER 3** *then walks off of the stage.)*

CHARACTER 7. *(Spitting out water and talking to herself.)* When I get my hands on that girl! *(She begins to walk up the escalator, looking down.)* Oh girlie! I seem to have left my purse up here, have you seen it? *(She gets to the top step before looking around.)* Oh dear! Oh my where have they gone? Winston? Winston, come help me at once! *(She waits expectantly for a reply but receives none. After a *few seconds she sighs, takes a deep breath in, plugs her nose with one hand, turns away from the audience, and thrusts her elbow and other arm straight out. There might be a blackout— and a loud splash.)*

End of Play

Atlas's Equal

by

Austin Hughes

ATLAS'S EQUAL was presented in a staged reading as part of the Thespian Playworks program at the 2015 Thespian Festival on June 27. Elise Kauzlaric was Director, Judy GeBauer served as Dramaturg, and Ellen Greetham served as Stage Manager. The cast was as follows:

ALEX . . . . Trevor Lown

ISOM . . . . C.J. Nickersom

HELEN PROCTOR . . . . Amelia Corrada

MIRANDA . . . . .Sydni Bringhurst

PARIS HALE . . . . .Dylan Schnabel

ALEXANDER WILLIAMS . . . . Blake Roberts

ATLAS'S EQUAL was originally produced at James Martin High School, directed by J'Mia Barrow. The cast was as follows:

ALEX . . . . Cameron Hayes

ISOM . . . . .Josh Jones

HELEN PROCTOR . . . . Molly Roberts

PARIS . . . . .Luke Lowrance

MIRANDA . . . . .Kayla Mattox

ALEXANDER WILLIAMS . . . . Gavin McGowan

ABOUT THE PLAYWRIGHT

A graduate of James W. Martin High School in Arlington, Texas, Austin Hughes has just completed his first year at the University of Iowa, double-majoring in English and Japanese with a minor in Theatre Arts. Of the Playworks experience, he said, "It truly opened my eyes. That one week really made a difference in my life, and I am so very thankful for that."

CHARACTERS

ALEX WILLIAMS – Son of Helen Proctor, age twelve

ISOM PROCTOR – African male, fourteen, adopted son of Helen Proctor

HELEN PROCTOR – Unmarried tavern owner, mid-twenties

PARIS BLACKBURN – British officer stationed in the colonies, mid-twenties

MIRANDA GOOD – Friend to the Proctor family, around sixteen

ALEXANDER WILLIAMS – Alex's father, around thirty

SETTING

Summer 1774, Boston, Massachusetts—roughly six months after the Boston Tea Party, and just after the enforcement of a new Quartering Act, part of the so-called "Intolerable Acts" passed by the British authorities in retaliation for the uprising. The law compelled colonists to provide food and housing for British troops stationed in their towns.

Scene One

*(Lights up on a small kitchen filled with a variety of wooden tools and furniture. One door leads to the tavern and bedrooms, and the other door leads to the back yard and rear entrance of the tavern. In the kitchen sits a rough-hewn wooden table with several tankards placed on top beside plates and spoons and a vase or pot with a motley bouquet standing in it. Four chairs surround the table, and a small wooden keg sits in one of the corners of the room. A stool, washboard and bucket sit somewhere within the room as well. The kitchen is clearly in great use and is extremely messy, but not filthy. It is deep night, and **ALEX** enters, creeping slowly. **ALEX** is an extremely childish and naïve boy who rarely sees beyond his own nose. He is clearly attempting to not be caught doing something, and he slithers in a few feet of the kitchen. He checks to see if the coast is clear and turns back to the entrance.)*

ALEX. *(Whispering.)* Come here!

*(After a brief pause, **ISOM** enters, creeping as well. **ISOM** somewhat makes up for the maturity **ALEX** lacks. He joins **ALEX** and the two titter softly for a moment—both giddy with excitement. They split and begin to search the room. Eventually **ALEX** observes the tankards sitting on the table, most of which are empty. However, **ALEX** finds what he is looking for and gestures fiercely to **ISOM**, bringing him over. **ALEX** hands him one of two tankards with enough left for a midnight swig. They smile at each other and press the mugs together—causing*

   a dull clang to ring through the air. They begin to drink deeply.)

HELEN. *(Calling from offstage.)* Alex? Where are you?!

   (The two boys look at each other—caught—and quickly set the tankards down as **HELEN** *enters from the front room. Hair tied up, she wears a smudged apron, a cleaning rag draped over her shoulder, and sweat from a long night's work.* **HELEN** *stares steadily at* **ALEX** *and* **ISOM** *who only give simultaneous, sheepish grins.)*

Alright, what are you two weasels up to? Know you not what time of day it is?

ALEX. Pray pardon us, mother. Our room grew most warm in this scorching summer, so we came down to cool ourselves. Nothing more.

HELEN. Nothing more?

ISOM. Aye, momma.

HELEN. Truly?

ALEX. Truly, mother.

   (HELEN *looks them over for a moment and then sees the tankards behind them.)*

HELEN. Aha—you lie! Now one of you speak the truth now, and the whipping shall be gentle.

   (The boys take her sly teasing at face value.)

ALEX. Spare us the whipping, mother. We pray your forgiveness… But just beware that this childish plot was all created by Isom's fault. I knew nothing of his sinister intentions 'til he offered me the tankard with his own hands—

ISOM. No, no, no, this was not by Isom's fault. Pray you hear me, momma! I were in a deep sleep, and Alex came to me in the dead of night—a whisperin' to me. He say to me "Isom, you and me, we creep down to the hearth and betray our poor momma's heart," and then he try to get me to sign the Devil's book—

ALEX. I never did no such thing!

ISOM. You lie, Devil, you lie!

HELEN. Silence your storytellin'. I'd sooner believe a boy cryin' wolf in the middle of the Boston Harbor. Now, I bid you tell the truth… You were after a swig of ale, weren't ya?

(*The two nod.*)

(*Beat; with a smile.*) Well, I'd be happy to serve ya. Sit you down.

(**HELEN** *situates* **ALEX** *and* **ISOM** *in chairs and clears the used tankards. She begins to spiffy up the table as if serving grown men and looks at the two of them.*)

What will you two be havin'?

ALEX AND ISOM. Ale!

HELEN. Cash on the barrelhead, sailors.

(**HELEN,** *although weary, puts on a show for her boys as she prepares them each a beer.*)

ALEX. How does your work fare, Mother?

HELEN. Quite well, thanks for askin'.

ISOM. Anyone peculiar come a-walkin' through the tavern?

HELEN. Nay. I'm still servin' the same beetle-headed fools. Why go and ask such a queer a question as that?

ALEX. Because the whole town's speakin'!

HELEN. Speakin' o' what?

ISOM. 'Bout what the Tories declared just a fortnight ago. The whole of the town is up in a stir about it.

HELEN. And what does the town say?

ALEX. They say there's trouble brewin'!

ISOM. They say the Tories'll drive us from Boston!

HELEN. And you two listened to such nonsense?

ALEX. 'Tis not nonsense, mother! William Edison told me so, and his word is sound as stone!

HELEN. William Edison also told you Isom was covered in dirt and could be washed clean. That boy's word is brittle as a newborn chick.

ISOM. There were no deceit in his words, momma! His father works on the harbor.

HELEN. What do the harbor and the truth share?

ALEX. A whole lot of Tories came off a big ship!

HELEN. So William Edison tells you?

ISOM. Aye, and others too!

HELEN. Well, I have yet to hear of any disruption in Boston, and no queer character has come 'round my tavern. Now you two quit your restlessness, and let no meddling words shake your mind lest you get to lyin' for sport like that William Edison.

ALEX. It be no lie, mother. Miranda told a similar tale.

ISOM. And Miranda cannot lie!

HELEN. I'd sooner you seek counsel in a mouser-cat than Miranda. At least the mouser would keep you from trouble. I love her dearly, but that girl will have you dreamin' of corruptions.

ALEX AND ISOM. But—

HELEN. Nay, children. Lay this talk of Tories and war to rest. Without thinkin' of such suspicions you might come to earn a decent night's rest. *(Off their looks; soothingly.)* All will be well. I would never allow it a different way.

ALEX. Boston will be well?

HELEN. *(With a smile.)* Aye.

ALEX. Truly?

HELEN. Truly, truly.

ALEX. And all our friends will be well?

HELEN. Aye.

ALEX. Truly?

HELEN. Truly, truly.

ISOM. Miranda as well?

HELEN. Aye, Miranda as well.

ALEX. And when Father returns—he will be well?

HELEN. *(Beat.)* Aye.

ALEX. Truly?

HELEN. Truly, truly. 'Tis as I said… All will be well. Now I bid you return to your bed.

ALEX. Will you be comin' to bed soon, mother?

HELEN. Soon as I wash me counters. Now, off with you.

> (**ALEX** *and* **ISOM** *begin to leave.*)

Forgotten something, have you?

> (**ALEX** *and* **ISOM** *turn around and hug their mother.*)

Good night.

ALEX AND ISOM. Good night.

> *(The two exit, and* **HELEN** *smiles to herself. She begins to clean out the boys' tankards, and sets them with the others to be used the following day. She begins to straighten up the kitchen, and as she does so, a knock sounds.)*

HELEN. *(Calling in, mistaken in her tiredness.)* Take yourselves to bed!

> *(Another much harsher knock is heard, and* **HELEN** *locates the true source of the sound. She steps up to the back door.)*

The tavern has shut its doors. Come back on the morrow at noon.

PARIS. I appear under orders of the British Crown. Release your door.

> (**HELEN** *does as she is told, and a strapping young man in uniform,* **PARIS,** *enters.)*

HELEN. Why do you come here? I know not what warrants this intrusion.

PARIS. It is as I said. I come to Boston from Britain. I be an officer of the Royal Army.

HELEN. Yes, I fathom that, but who bid you come *here?*

PARIS. Are you not familiar with the decree made just a fortnight ago?

HELEN. Aye, I heard of yet another act passed by the Crown, but in all truth, I chose to neglect it.

PARIS. Where is the owner of this property—your husband? Perhaps he will lend a more capable ear.

HELEN. Myself am the owner of this property. These are the only ears available. Now why do you invade my home?

PARIS. The decree you neglect is reason for me being here, madam. I require a temporary apartment.

> *(He hands her a piece of parchment, and she scans it.* **HELEN** *cannot read.)*

The Quarterin' Act warrants it.

HELEN. Quarterin' Act, I recall… A bucket of crap, that is. Ever since some loggerheads went and wasted your tea you've become a scaly bunch. I cannot allow one of you to sleep under me roof.

PARIS. Is that so? *(Disregarding her.)* Where is your husband, madam? I'd sooner take conflict from him than a wom—

HELEN. For the final time, this is my property. You'll take as much conflict as I give. And as for a husband, I have none.

PARIS. Then how do you come to own this ale house?

HELEN. My father. I was his only, and when he died, the tavern became mine. *(With reverence.)* Aye. The Proctor Tavern, and that's me. Helen Proctor.

PARIS. *(With a smile.)* Helen is your name?

HELEN. Yes, what of it?

PARIS. Nothing. I am Paris Blackburn—

HELEN. I don't recall askin' for names. Now, I want you out of my tavern, so I can get back to workin'. So I bid you take your fancy Quarterin' Act and stay at William Edison's house. He'd relish roomin' with you.

PARIS. Look you, I pray you forgive me for my surliness. I am simply doing what was bid of me, and now I swear that I come to you without fangs. Can we not start again on a much loftier note?

HELEN. *(Softening.)* Aye.

PARIS. I am Paris Blackburn.

HELEN. I heard the first announcement… Sit you down.

> (**PARIS** *sits at the table, and* **HELEN** *begins to serve him as she would any other customer—wiping down the table and so forth.*)

Aye, you are a fribble. First you come bargin' in here demandin' a bed and food of me, and then you choose to treat a woman with tenderness.

PARIS. Is that not how all women yearn to be treated?

HELEN. Aye, but I should have no need to go requestin' respect—especially on my own land.

PARIS. As I said, I apologize.

HELEN. Yes, Mr. Blackburn, and I accept it. You drink?

PARIS. What type of men do not drink?

HELEN. The clever ones.

PARIS. You speak from experience?

HELEN. Aye, remember me tellin' you my father owned this tavern? He used to lay waste to himself with drink, and he'd be stuck dumb for days. I'd run the place in his stead 'til he'd "go back to Jesus."

PARIS. The obscenity of a tavern does not quite seem the proper place for a woman.

HELEN. Yes, I have a different something down below, but I am capable of runnin' this place just as well as my father once did. *(She hands him the drink.)*

PARIS. Thank you. *(Observing her.)* You are a strange one. I've heard tales of the women in the colonies from fellow soldiers, especially when I was posted in England. It's all lore beyond here.

HELEN. Is it now?

PARIS. Aye, I've heard a diverse bunch of myths—stories sayin' you're either harlots or criminals, but you— *(A quiet laugh.)* You contradict all I've heard.

HELEN. How's that?

PARIS. You're a spitfire.

HELEN. I'd prefer to go without spittin'. It's unladylike.

PARIS. That's what I mean… That and you're beautiful—much more so than any other lady I've encountered both here and in England.

HELEN. Surely you jest.

PARIS. Oh no, I do not jest—not ever. I do not want to be mistaken…and I do not want you to mistake me.

HELEN. Ahh, and come here, I thought all you Tories despised us colonists.

PARIS. Who could despise a face of such beauty?

HELEN. I could surprise you. I've my share of enemies.

PARIS. You do not surprise me at all. Surely, jealousy is a plague whenever you come about.

HELEN. Are you simply pot-valiant or does this goodly speech have a value?

PARIS. As I said… I do not want to be mistaken.

HELEN. I see… Well, apart from your scaly behavior of earlier, your honesty has left me a tad softened. I'll abide your silly little act. You can stay in my tavern for the time bein'. There won't be any more of the likes of you, will there?

PARIS. As of now? Nay.

HELEN. I'll be showin' you to your room then. You're fortunate we have a spare.

PARIS. We? Are you not married?

HELEN. I have children. Two to be truthful.

PARIS. I see. Aye, you are a fribble. First you act as though your heart is made of stone, and now you choose to reveal your tenderness to me.

HELEN. Quiet your mouth or it'll be back to the streets. Now I bid you follow me.

>(**HELEN** *leads* **PARIS** *off stage into the tavern entrance, and the lights fade.*)

Scene Two

(Nine days have passed. Lights up on **HELEN,** *who kneels at the washboard and pail, scrubbing clothes.* **ALEX** *and* **ISOM** *enter.)*

ALEX. We prepared the mash, mother.

ISOM. It be sittin' in the cellar now.

HELEN. Good then, go bring more hop to the loft. It will be time for dinner soon. 'Fore you go, run yourselves to Paris's apartment and bid him come to me.

ALEX AND ISOM. Aye.

*(***ALEX** *and* **ISOM** *race away to the tavern, and a knock sounds from the back door.)*

HELEN. It's the Sabbath. We're not openin' our doors.

MIRANDA. I'm not some crusty, old drunk. It's I—Miranda!

HELEN. Oh, let you come. The door is open.

*(***MIRANDA** *enters.)*

MIRANDA. Why hold that from me then?

HELEN. I knew you'd come a-bargin' in without any manners.

MIRANDA. I pray your forgiveness! Good morrow, Helen!

HELEN. Good morrow, Miranda. Your face has been rare of late.

MIRANDA. You know I can't come paradin' through here as I please. The town already believes you to have signed the Devil's book. I can't have them thinkin' me to be his harlot too.

HELEN. Aye, I know it. How do you fare?

MIRANDA. I fare well… And what of you? I heard you've got a Tory in that spare apartment of yours.

HELEN. Aye. That be true.

MIRANDA. *(With sudden enthusiasm.)* So what is life with a Tory like? Is he kind to ya? Does he speak about layin' waste to the Colonies? Does he ever threaten your children?

HELEN. No.

MIRANDA. Oh… Then what sort of Tory is he? I heard o' the ones down at the barracks. They aren't too kind.

HELEN. He's kind to me—more kind than any man I knew. It's a shame. I could never find a more decent man than he.

MIRANDA. I pray I had your fortune. I simply cannot choose.

HELEN. *(Dryly.)* Surely, you cannot.

MIRANDA. You cannot fathom what Benedict say to me earlier this mornin'. He invited me on a stroll with him.

HELEN. And what say you?

MIRANDA. I had to decline. Mark this! He only seeks Betty's envy, so he plotted to have her see me and him a walkin' this mornin'. I saw him clear through like a bucket o' ale.

HELEN. Ale has an amber tint. That don't seem like a clear sight to me.

MIRANDA. I speak true, I tell ya. Oh! And mark this as well! Betty's been a-glarin' at me in church too! Envy's a sin, ya know.

HELEN. I pray God forgive her then.

(PARIS *enters.*)

PARIS. Good morrow.

HELEN. *(Warmly.)* Good morrow.

PARIS. Who is this young woman?

HELEN. *(To* MIRANDA.*)* Go on.

MIRANDA. *(Wide eyed.)* Me name's Miranda…

PARIS. Pleasure to meet you.

MIRANDA. Aye.

HELEN. Did Alex and Isom speak o' dinner to you?

PARIS. Yes.

HELEN. Good then. Now, would you mind helpin' the boys carry the hop to the loft?

PARIS. Can you not bid the dark one to assist you? And what of Alex—?

HELEN. Alex and **ISOM** are already there but the load is much too large even for the two of them. Now I bid you please—show them how a man is to work.

PARIS. *(Flirtatiously, like a dutiful husband.)* Aye, Goody. *(He exits.)*

MIRANDA. Goody! Be you two in wedlock!?

HELEN. Nay, Miranda. 'Twas only a jest.

MIRANDA. Oh, good then. That man is a smug bull fit for any woman. Why, he has me sweatin' like a stallion, Helen. I speak true.

HELEN. Quell your heat, Miranda. There be no interest from Paris in you.

MIRANDA. Well, tear down my fanciful dreams then… Or is it that you dote on a Tory?

HELEN. Well… Yes, I do.

MIRANDA. Helen, I smile at the sight of you dotin', but Paris allies with the Crown. Do you not fault? And what of Alexander—

HELEN. *(Cutting her off.)* I do not fault anything. He stay with me eight days now, and shown me more kindness than the whole of Boston. Can I not dote on the giver of such prodigious affection? Judge me not!

MIRANDA. I judge you not. I worry for you. I pray your life does not become the center of some obscene scandal is all.

HELEN. I thank you for your worry. But my doting is only such. Doting. I have no intentions of marryin' him, and his stay is only temporary. Worry not.

MIRANDA. Aye, I shall worry no more. You have my word.

HELEN. Your word is worth as much as a fish to the ocean. Now, shall you join us for dinner?

MIRANDA. Nay, I cannot. John is meetin' me at the harbor. I would like some ale, however!

HELEN. Ale? You still choose drink on the Sabbath?

MIRANDA. The Sabbath is a fancy word for another day. Fill me tankard to the brim!

HELEN. Aye, I hear you. *(Calling.)* Boys, I bid you come to me. Dinner is ready.

> *(**ALEX**, **ISOM**, and **PARIS** enter.)*

Alex, throw the water in that bucket out, and Isom set me clothes out to dry.

> *(**ALEX** and **ISOM** begin to do as they're told, but **ISOM** sees **MIRANDA** and is awestruck.)*

ISOM. G-good morrow, Miranda.

MIRANDA. Good morrow, Isom!

> *(**ALEX** tugs on **ISOM**, and the two exit through the back door.)*

That one likes me, he does.

HELEN. Yes, but you'd best not wound his heart, Miranda.

MIRANDA. I shall do no such thing... He *is* a bit too dark for me. *(Beat.)* What shade you think our babies would be?

HELEN. I bid you go the harbor, Miranda.

MIRANDA. Aye, I'm goin'. *(Exiting.)* I'll be back on the morrow!

> *(**MIRANDA** exits.)*

PARIS. She is awful queer.

HELEN. Believe you me. Some days I cannot fathom her.

> *(**ALEX** and **ISOM** return.)*

Sit you both down.

> *(**ALEX** and **ISOM** sit, and **HELEN** begins to pour stew into the bowls in front of them. **ALEX** begins to eat.)*

Stop, you! Have you no manners? Give your thanks to God.

ALEX. *(Looking up.)* Thank you, God.

 (He continues eating, and **ISOM** *follows suit.)*

HELEN. That stew will rebel in your stomach if you carry on that way.

PARIS. *(Smiling at* **ALEX.***)* Leave him. How else is a man to eat?

 *(***ALEX*** smiles back at* **PARIS.** **ISOM** *smiles at* **PARIS** *as well, and* **PARIS***'s smile immediately fades.* **HELEN** *watches them eat for a moment and then seats herself.)*

HELEN. Good then.

 (She dips her spoon in her bowl and lifts it to her mouth just as a knock is heard. **HELEN** *rises from her seat without the men skipping a beat in their meal. Calling.)*

Our door is closed. Come back on the morrow—

 *(***ALEXANDER*** enters, and the scene freezes.* **HELEN** *is struck in the chest and cannot speak nor move, and* **PARIS** *is dumbfounded.)*

ALEX. *(Rushing past* **HELEN.***)* Father! *(The two embrace.)* How do you fare?

ALEXANDER. Now that I see you again I fare well. What of you, my son?

ALEX. All is well! You've returned!

ALEXANDER. Aye.

ALEX. *(To* **HELEN.***)* It's just as you said.

HELEN. Yes…

ALEXANDER. Now, what dinner is there?

ALEX. *(Leading his father to the table.)* Mother has made stew, and she has tarts for after.

ALEXANDER. *(Sitting in* **HELEN***'s previous seat.)* I look forward to it. *(To* **HELEN.***)* Don't stand so dumb, Helen. Serve me.

HELEN. *(Coldly.)* The stew is in that bowl.

ALEXANDER. Good then.

(He begins to eat, and **ALEX** *returns to his seat and does the same. Through his consumption.)* Where be the tarts?

HELEN. The oven.

ALEXANDER. Good then. Fetch me some ale, woman.

*(***HELEN** *silently does as she's told.)*

PARIS. *(Breaking his pensive silence.)* You ignore me?

ALEXANDER. *(Without looking from his food.)* I shall not acknowledge a lowly Tory.

ALEX. No father. Mark this! Paris is a kind Tory. He take me to the market and he—

ALEXANDER. Silence your childish nonsense! Any Tory be a hellish Tory.

PARIS. Only your kind would know the look of hell's bowels.

ALEXANDER. You wish to test my familiarity with hell?

PARIS. I wish for you to be civil.

ALEXANDER. *(Starting calmly but then angrily.)* I'll be civil soon as you and your devilish crown are ripped from this world!

HELEN. Stop this! I'll have none of this disruption! Alex and Isom, I bid you go to your room.

*(***ALEX** *and* **ISOM** *scurry away without a word.* **HELEN** *hands* **ALEX***ander a tankard of beer and stands beside him.)*

(Off **PARIS***'s look.)* Why do you stare at me so?

PARIS. *(With a flash of anger.)* You've filled my ears with lies!

ALEXANDER. What ever she spoke to you weren't truth.

PARIS. *(To* **HELEN***.)* You said—

HELEN. *(To* **PARIS***.)* I know what I said, and I spoke in truth. Now, I beg of you place away your anger and wait outside. I will conceal no more… I need speak with him—alone.

PARIS. *(He looks at the two.)* Very well.

*(***PARIS** *exits through the back door, and* **ALEX***ander moves over to the door—making sure* **PARIS** *has*

left. He then turns with a smile to **HELEN** *who stands at a distance both physically and mentally.* **ALEX***ander nears* **HELEN**, *and* **HELEN** *steps away, grabbing a broom and beginning to sweep.)*

ALEXANDER. Why do you flee from my touch?

HELEN. I do not flee. The floor is sullied.

ALEXANDER. *(Teasingly.)* I cannot blink it. Have you gone daft with sloth?

HELEN. I have gone daft with solitude.

ALEXANDER. *(Beat; off her tone.)* I think my return would be the cause of more joy.

HELEN. As do I. But can a moment of joy fill this eighteen-month your departure?

ALEXANDER. *(Soothingly.)* I share in your hurt. Separation is many a nail in my heart, but I beg you rejoice in our reunion. Time will sear us no more.

> (**ALEXANDER** *approaches* **HELEN** *from behind and slowly places his arms around her.* **HELEN** *grows uncomfortable and pulls herself away.)*

Enough! I'll not have your contempt! Why does my son rush to me while you choose to shame me?

HELEN. I do not shame you. A person bids their own shame. I only wonder why you choose your return now.

ALEXANDER. It matters not. Hell is upon us.

HELEN. In what way?

ALEXANDER. Know you nothing? You cannot blink it any longer! A Tory rests beneath this very roof and many more in all of Boston! The country is bounding towards war fast as the Devil's descent to hell, and yet you play yourself blind!

HELEN. I know the black state of things, but I still know not why you reveal yourself with such innocence… I thought you dead! You said you would be a-headin' to New York for talk of revolution, yet you return without havin' sent no letter—no mark of your life—while I suffer under thoughts of your silent passin' …

ALEXANDER. *(He comes to acknowledge her emotions.)* Yes… I pray your forgiveness, I do. I know you worry so.

HELEN. I do not worry for my own bein'. I worry for our son that everyday looks to you.

ALEXANDER. Yes, yes, I pray forgiveness, I pray… But this be no time for quarrelin' …I return because I fear for the safety of both you and our son.

HELEN. *(A light scoff of incredulity.)* Truly now?

ALEXANDER. *(Earnestly.)* Aye… And with that Tory away I bid you pack our belongings and make the pilgrimage with me to God's protection.

HELEN. What nonsense is this?

ALEXANDER. This be no nonsense! …We will flee Boston.

HELEN. And flee where? If providence is dead here, where else does it live?

ALEXANDER. Pennsylvania. Delegates of all colonies will be there tryin' to sort through this madness. If war is to strike, we will best brave it there.

HELEN. Pennsylvania is many a mile away. Must we leave?

ALEXANDER. We must and we will. Now, I've returned to you to pack our things and bring us to safety, and you will come. We shall never know solitude again.

HELEN. *(Beat.)* What am I to do?

ALEXANDER. *(He steps to her; reasserting his forgotten power.)* You will do as I say.

> **(ALEXANDER** *walks past* **HELEN** *without another word and exits to the bedrooms.* **HELEN** *stands alone as lights fade.)*

Scene Three

> *(Lights up on the empty kitchen on the following day.* **ALEX** *and* **ISOM** *rush inside while playing a game—***ALEX** *shooting an imaginary rifle at* **ISOM.** *)*

ALEX. I've shot you. Why do you not faint?

ISOM. I tire of this game. Why must I forever play Indian?

ALEX. *(He observes the skin of his arm for a moment.)* Well I cannot play Indian.

> *(***PARIS** *enters.)*

(Excitedly.) Good morning, Mr. Paris!

PARIS. Good morning, Alex.

ALEX. It's still early, but when noon comes, shall we go to the market?

PARIS. Nay, I cannot. I am to meet my fellow officers.

> *(***PARIS** *sits in a chair, and* **ALEX** *does the same.)*

(To **ISOM.***)* Slave, fetch me a tankard of beer.

ALEX. *(***ISOM** *stands truly befuddled. A slight pause.)* Isom! Fetch him some ale!

ISOM. O-oh. *(He obeys.)*

ALEX. *(Pause.)* Are you and Father friends?

PARIS. Do ever God and the Devil feast with one another?

ALEX. I suppose they do not… But they once did—did they not?

PARIS. Aye, you speak true. But you will come to find that all hope in this world is equaled by despair. Miracle and disaster loom alike.

ALEX. Oh…

PARIS. *(***ISOM** *returns and hands him a tankard.)* Have you forgotten your arithmetic? I count one person more.

ISOM. Oh. *(He begins to go.)* I will just—

PARIS. Nay, do not strain your thoughts any further. He will have what remains of mine. Stand you there. *(He *drinks—puts his feet on the table; to* **ISOM**.) Why do you not entertain us? I bid you sing one of your Barbados songs.

ISOM. I know not what you mean. I cannot utter a single note, sir.

PARIS. Surely, you can. I've heard a slave sing many a time. Go on then.

ALEX. *(Putting his feet on the table.)* Do not stand so dumb. He bids you sing.

ISOM. I cannot—

PARIS. (**PARIS** *slams his tankard down.*) Enough. Now, I bid you hand this tankard over.

ALEX. (**ISOM** *does as he's told. Pause.*) I command you hold this tankard to my lips so that I may drink.

>(**PARIS** *laughs.*)

ISOM. What—?

ALEX. I bid you do it.

>(**ISOM** *hesitates but does as he's told and* **ALEX** *begins to drink.* **PARIS**'s *laughter rings out.*)

HELEN. *(Entering.)* What obscene practice is this? I bid this madness stop!

>(*They stop. To* **ALEX**.)

What say you on this, Alex?

ALEX. We only bid Isom sing.

HELEN. That weren't singing. Treatin' him like a house slave for sport? That be singin' now? I bid you go outside, and pray his forgiveness. Then you two will tend the fire of the brew. I will deal with your foolishness another hour. Go, away with you both.

>(**ALEX** *and* **ISOM** *quickly exit through the back door, and* **HELEN** *turns to* **PARIS**, *who simply glowers at her.*)

Have you gone daft?

PARIS. *(Matter-of-fact.)* I pray your forgiveness. I thought him a slave, so I asked him to sing a Barbados song.

HELEN. He be no slave from Barbados! I did not purchase him as I would a sack o' flour. I found that child abandoned in some black night—cryin' out for mercy no one was givin'. With God my witness, I've cared for him since. He been raised no different than you or I. That boy is family.

PARIS. *(Unsoftened.)* Is that so?

HELEN. What demon ails you?

PARIS. It is no demon so much as it is a blemish on my conscience. Your family is larger than you first told.

HELEN. You are mistaken. Alexander is no family.

PARIS. Aye?

HELEN. *(Primly.)* Aye. Together we only bring a child into this world. There be no wedlock.

PARIS. *(Pause.)* Why conceal him?

HELEN. It were not concealment then… I thought him gone—never to return. But even if I knew the precise hour of his reappearance, it would matter not… I do not love him.

PARIS. Do you tell me true?

HELEN. Aye. He even bid me go to Pennsylvania with him; however, I think I will not.

PARIS. *(He smiles—truly impressed.)* Surely women lust for such confidences. You be a true marvel like that of the three brave men of the furnace. *(A reference to a miracle described in the Book of Daniel, illustrating the power of faith over corruption.* **PARIS** *places his arms around* **HELEN** *and feels her.)*

HELEN. Why thank you, but I am no marvel such as that. I am only a woman.

PARIS. A woman unlike any other. There be so much strength behind your delicate face—so much sensuality and passion. Why, if a man holds up the earth then surely a woman holds the moon.

HELEN. *(Losing her composure.)* Aye, but surely a woman gave birth to such a man to begin with.

> *(***PARIS*** *suddenly pulls her close, and they look at each other for a moment, barely breathing. They kiss.* ***ALEX*** *enters. He sees the two, and quickly exits.)*

(Nudging **PARIS** *away; still aroused.)* Wait, I do not wish for my children to see.

PARIS. Aye, then let us go where they cannot.

> *(***PARIS*** *begins to lead* ***HELEN*** *off stage towards the empty tavern.* ***HELEN*** *hesitates for a moment, the two exchanging a brief look, but inevitably she follows* ***PARIS*** *in. A moment passes with only the deserted kitchen as lights fade off. A knock sounds. Lights fade up.)*

MIRANDA. Helen, 'tis Miranda. I said I'd be back on the morrow, and here I am… Helen? (She enters and sees the empty kitchen.) Helen? …The single time I come find you outside the—

> *(***PARIS*** *enters—mopping his brow.)*

Oh, good morrow, Paris.

PARIS. *(Quickly exiting through the back door.)* Good morrow, Miranda.

MIRANDA. *(The officer gone, she shrugs off the encounter.)* Helen? Oh, Helen? *(Heading towards the tavern entrance.)* Where are you—?

> *(***HELEN*** *enters like a ghost, and stares* ***MIRANDA*** *in the face.* ***MIRANDA*** *jumps.* ***HELEN*** *quickly circumvents* ***MIRANDA*** *and begins to compulsively clean and straighten the kitchen.)*

You frightened me! Poppin' out like a ghostly thing! What say you to that? *(No answer.)* Will you not answer me? Has somethin' gone on that I know not of? *(Beat; believing to have connected the dots.)* Oh, I see… He gave you a flourish, did he not!? Speak true, Helen. Was it

like a breathin' dream? *(No answer.)* I bid you answer
me! You and Paris lie together, do you not?

HELEN. *(Pause. Lifelessly.)* Aye.

MIRANDA. Oh, Helen! I almost cannot fathom it! *He* had
his way with you!

HELEN. Aye, he did.

MIRANDA. *(Her ignorance turns to concern.)* That's a good
thing. Is it not? Helen, some hide behind drink, but
you hide behind your broom. I bid you stop—!

HELEN. Do not lay a hand on me! I am sullied!

MIRANDA. Helen...

HELEN. I bid him only give me a soft word and a kiss,
but it were much more. I said nay, but I suppose half
through it I turned... I did not fight, and I fathom
it. I truly do, Miranda. I fathom it! ...He were not at
fault... My own mother passed givin' life to me, and
I knew not why my father hated me so... It was not
until Alex show signs within my belly that I knew it...
I pray to God Alex come to me a boy—I pray and I
pray—because what good is a woman? And I fathom it
now! A woman chooses her own sufferin'—she lets it
within her whether it be familiar or foreign—and she
settles for it... She settles... And I am a woman. I am
no different... I settle...

(**MIRANDA** *embraces* **HELEN**. *Lights fade.*)

Scene Four

(It is now night. Lights up on **ALEXANDER,** *who sits at the table—throwing back a tankard of ale. His sobriety is slowly edging away, but he has yet to lose himself. His brooding is the only thread tethering himself together.)*

ALEXANDER. HELEN!

(She scurries in. It's clear she has been waiting hand and foot on him. With a sour undertone:)

Fetch me more ale.

HELEN. I think it best you retire from this. This be your fifth—

ALEXANDER. *(An edge on his voice.)* I think it best you obey me!

*(***HELEN** *does as she is told. She hands the tankard to him. He drinks deeply but leaves remains.)*

HELEN. Why do you drink so? Has something happened?

ALEXANDER. Yes… A great pain is walking me, Helen. For I have gone and lost a thing so near and dear to me that my insides shudder at the thought of it.

HELEN. What do you speak of? Perhaps I can search about and find it.

ALEXANDER. *(Pause. He looks at her.)* I have lost you. *(He holds out the partially filled tankard to her.)* What say you to that?

HELEN. *(She takes it. Almost guiltily.)* I'd say you are mistaken. *(She drinks.)*

ALEXANDER. Is that so…

*(***HELEN** *hands the tankard back to* **ALEXANDER** *and he finishes it off. He sets it on the table, and* **HELEN** *reaches for it.)*

Nay, no more drink. We will talk.

HELEN. *(She sits.)* Talk of what?

ALEXANDER. You and I.

HELEN. What of us?

ALEXANDER. *(A beat while he attempts to compose himself.)* What is your understanding of me?

HELEN. Why must we talk of such nonsense—?

ALEXANDER. 'Tis not nonsense! I— ...I only wish to know your honest thought, and I know you will answer me true... Now, what is your understanding of me?

HELEN. *(Not knowing what to say, silence and unease sets in.)* I— ... I believe you to be the—the father of my only... I believe you to—to be a good man at heart, I surely do. I...

ALEXANDER. Go on—

HELEN. I... I know not what else must be said.

ALEXANDER. Do you love me?

HELEN. *(As if she did not hear the question.)* I beg your pardon—

ALEXANDER. Hear me! ...Do you, Helen, love me?

HELEN. I—

> *(The words do not come. Pause.* ALEX*ander stares intently at her with aching eyes.)*

I—

(Overlapping his next line.) I do! I do love you!

ALEXANDER. *(Overlapping.)* Why do you falter!? If you falter then you do not speak true, and that is all I ask of you! Speak true!

HELEN. How may I speak true, when I must suffer shame for my honesty?

ALEXANDER. You said yourself to me a person bids their own shame!

HELEN. Yes, and I shame myself for the truth I bear.

ALEXANDER. Then it is a lie. You do not love me.

HELEN. How may I love what I cannot lay eyes on?

ALEXANDER. Cease such foolishness! You loved me then and you love me yet! I've spent many a night away from you, and my love for you has never waned. Do not play yourself differently!

HELEN. I do not play any different from you! The crosses you and I carried were far from the same! When I bore Alex outside of wedlock, I was the target of disgrace and ignominy while you pranced freely from town to town. With your time away you know not of the trials and tribulations I myself faced—unsupported!

ALEXANDER. I have always left with you and young Alexander in mind! Do not draw me so selfish! You speak as if life have always treated me with comfort.

HELEN. And who is the judge of discomfort? A man who knows it not, or a woman who lives it?

ALEXANDER. Know your place, bitch! Do not give me such surly speech!

HELEN. Any speech of my heart were always surly in your eyes!

ALEXANDER. Because you speak as a selfish harlot would! I have done naught but given you the respect of a proper goodwife even without wedlock, and yet you treat me so. You shame me, yet I have only ever loved you!

HELEN. Yes, well your love could cause the sun to shiver!

ALEXANDER. End this heartless speech! I know not what warrants such bitterness from you! You have always loved me, and I know it in confidence. Notwithstanding there be no wedlock, I know it! Notwithstanding your frigidity, I know it to be so! Because even with the passage of time you love me yet! Now, confess it! Confess!

HELEN. I do not... I could never love such a volatile presence! And I could *never* give my heart to a fair-weather husband!

ALEXANDER. *(Beat.)* So it is I who does the Devil's work, and you be my saint. You seek to expel Him from me by speaking true? Then let us speak true... I know of you and the Tory.

HELEN. I know not what you mean.

ALEXANDER. I grow tired of this evasion! If you won't speak truth, then I will pry it from you using God's fingers! *(Violently.)* ALEX!

> **(ALEX** *enters. It is likely he has heard this entire confrontation.)*

ALEX. Yes?

ALEXANDER. Stay you there. *(To* **HELEN.** *)* Now, answer me. Did you have your way with the Tory?

HELEN. …I did not.

ALEXANDER. Did you have your way with the Tory!?

HELEN. I did not!

ALEXANDER. I see… Alex, tell me once more what you lay eyes on this mornin'.

ALEX. *(Unsure of what to do, he glances at his mother.)* I—

ALEXANDER. Do not look at her! Tell me!

ALEX. …I saw mother and Mr. Paris—kissin' …

ALEXANDER. *(To* **HELEN.** *)* Yet you did not have your way with him!

HELEN. I did not—!

ALEXANDER. *(His first true explosion.)* Enough! You've forsaken the love we share, and I truly cannot fathom it! I have done naught but deliver us from peril and seek to defend the sanctity of this house! I only pray for its peace and tranquility and to see my son grow to walk like a man! In this hellish time I have remained devoted to your very existence, and my mind has never strayed from your needs. My world is you—I have only taken breath for you… Yet you torture and shame me… Why? …What say you to that, Helen?

HELEN. *(Beat.)* I'd say you'll make a fair wife one day.

> **(ALEXANDER** *glares at* **HELEN.** *He slaps her harshly, and quickly pins her against the table— holding her arm behind her and her head down on*

the table. **HELEN** *cries out but she does not shed a tear. She is almost stoic.)*

ALEXANDER. You will give me respect!

HELEN. Earn it.

(*He twists her arm.*)

ALEX. Stop it—!

ALEXANDER. (*Mercilessly.*) Silence, child!

HELEN. So you would strike me? …Before the eyes of our own child?!

(**ALEXANDER** *considers this. He releases* **HELEN**, *but his rage does not subside. He angrily exits— laying waste to whatever is within arm's reach.* **HELEN** *is barely holding herself together. She surveys the damage and then, with an outward calm, she begins to clean.* **ALEX** *watches for a few beats.*)

ALEX. Where did father go?

HELEN. I know not. I'd ask God myself, but I believe He is angry with me… Where is Isom?

ALEX. In bed.

HELEN. Good then. Now, I bid you go to your room and sleep. You boys must remember to add yeast to the brew on the morrow—

ALEX. (*Indignantly.*) No.

HELEN. (*Ignoring his tone.*) Alex, do not play such games. Take yourself to bed.

ALEX. No, woman. I want to see Father.

HELEN. And I spoke true when I said I know not where he went now—

ALEX. But you are a liar! You lie to father!

HELEN. Alex—

ALEX. Tell me where he is!

HELEN. I know not—

(**ALEX** *slaps his mother.* **HELEN** *is shocked, then hurt.* **ALEX** *sees her change in expression and his face softens.* **HELEN***'s long-repressed emotions are suddenly revived.*)

(*Almost inaudibly.*) Go to bed.

ALEX. Mother—

HELEN. (*Erupting, with a voice* **ALEX** *has never heard.*) AWAY WITH YOU!

(**ALEX** *exits, leaving* **HELEN** *visibly trembling with profound emotion. She sinks into a chair and stares at her hands. Finally, she cries. The lights fade to black.*)

Scene Five

(Three days have passed. The kitchen is now extremely, sadly, tidy. **PARIS** *enters from the tavern and takes a seat at the table. He is puzzled by the emptiness of the room, and soon* **ALEX***ander enters from the back door. The two appraise each other.)*

PARIS. Good morrow.

ALEXANDER. Why do you sit here? Have you no business outside our home?

PARIS. Helen bid me come here.

ALEXANDER. *(Chuckling darkly to himself.)* So she speaks now?

PARIS. As of now, yes. This be the third day she's held her tongue. A fiery woman she is.

ALEXANDER. Do not speak so kindly of her. She will surely burn you.

PARIS. You still cannot be civil?

ALEXANDER. Civility means nothing in hell.

PARIS. If this gentle speech be hell, then I pray one day I reach heaven's doors.

ALEXANDER. Scum like you will never know of heaven.

PARIS. Aye, then neither shall you... You cry that the side I stand for is aligned with the Devil himself? You only soothe yourself. Who has never claimed to do God's work, for his own purpose?

*(***HELEN*** enters.)*

Ahh, Helen. Shall you speak?

ALEXANDER. What of supper? This table is bare as though we were beggars. Answer me!

HELEN. There will be no supper. We will talk.

ALEXANDER. After three days your silence, you bend to your whim and suddenly speak? You capricious whore—

PARIS. Silence. Let her speak.

ALEXANDER. You will not order me as you would a woman. She is mine—

HELEN. I bid you stop! We will talk, or may God himself smite me where I am!

(They stop at her conviction.)

ALEXANDER. *(Beat.)* Very well then. What will we talk of?

HELEN. *(To* **PARIS.***)* Paris— …You must leave here now.

PARIS. What do you mean?

HELEN. It is as I said. I pray that you leave here at this very moment. Now.

PARIS. Helen, I know not why you speak this—

HELEN. Because you are a detestable man. I have seen you through smiles and treachery, and I will play your game no longer. You do not love me. You love whatever visions come to you at night, and I cannot turn myself fanciful!

PARIS. Helen I truly do love you. If this devilish man of yours has planted seeds of suspicion within you, let you rip them from your thoughts of me now!

HELEN. You've sown your own suspicious seeds! Now, I bid you leave me be!

PARIS. *(More harshly.)* If I must leave, then I shall leave, but I bid you come with me. War is nigh, and the Crown will prevail, but if you remain here you may very well perish! *(More gently.)* I only worry for your safety… Helen, I have known you—

HELEN. Be gone!

PARIS. *(Receding into his anger.)* After all that I have done for you, you will turn from me? After all of the delicate affection and kindness I have shown you, you choose to shatter it and cut into me? I am required by law to remain here, and yet you banish me? Surely this is a jest!

HELEN. This is no jest… Do not mistake me…

PARIS. Mark this: When we ride upon Boston atop a pale horse, I will look for you… This tavern will be the first thing I set fire to. Beware my words.

(He gets in her face. **ALEXANDER** *rises.)* Do not mistake *me!*

(**PARIS** *exits. Silence.* **ALEXANDER** *goes to* **HELEN**.)

ALEXANDER. I was first unaware of your intentions, but now I know. You've done away with your foolishness, and you've repented these three days… I forgive you.

(**ALEXANDER** *goes to kiss her. She stops him.*)

HELEN. *(Simply.)* No. *(Beat.)* You must leave as well.

ALEXANDER. You pull from me yet? Do you mean to incite my rage?

HELEN. Aye! And you can rage about outside because just as Paris did, you will leave!

ALEXANDER. I will do no such thing—

HELEN. This is my property! You do not own a lick of it, so be gone!

ALEXANDER. I do not own this land, but I own you, Helen. You are mine!

HELEN. I am not yours, I am not Paris's, I am not anyone's! I am not land, Alexander! I am a woman, and I am my own!

ALEXANDER. And what is a woman worth but on her own? You wish to stand so tall alone, but if you go such a way you will fall without my support!

HELEN. What support do you speak of? You leave and return. You leave and return. You leave and you return! There is no support, unless it is I who cannot feel it!

ALEXANDER. Then you be an ungrateful woman, Helen!

HELEN. No… I am not ungrateful. I am exhausted!

ALEXANDER. *(Truly pained.)* We are to go to Pennsylvania together! We may own another tavern there, is that not what you want? Why do you thwart me at every turn like some crazed chapel ghost?

HELEN. Because I cannot go with you and rest soundly, knowing that I will continue to suffer for what you cannot endure.

ALEXANDER. You do not know the cross I bear!

HELEN. Because you have none! I carry your burdens for you, and I have broken beneath them! I do not wish to feel your pain for you any longer. I will tear my suffering from yours, and if as a woman I will perish alone, then so be it! I will gladly face this coming war without you. I will stand myself in the middle of the street and be trampled by a thousand horses of war! I will gladly let my flesh burn as my tavern goes up in flames, and I will swallow my own bitterness and anguish under whatever intolerable act must be passed next—all if it means that the agony I feel is mine and mine alone! I will suffer under you no more…

ALEXANDER. *(He steadily looks at her for a moment.)* You may be alone then. I will pine for you no longer, and I shall leave if that be your dearest hope… But I will have my son.

HELEN. No you will not!

ALEXANDER. If I am to leave, I shall take him with me! I will not leave him with you to be trampled under the Crown!

HELEN. You will not—!

ALEXANDER. *(Advancing towards her.)* I will!

HELEN. Wait, you!

> **(ALEXANDER** *holds his position.)*

…He will be a man soon… He may make this decision for himself as a man, and I shall respect it—whatever it may be… But will you?

ALEXANDER. *(He truly thinks of this. Long beat.)* I shall.

HELEN. Truly?

ALEXANDER. I said I shall!

HELEN. Good then… I will fetch him—

ALEXANDER. You will not. ALEX!

ALEX. *(A moment passes, and* **ALEX** *enters.)* Is supper ready?

ALEXANDER. Nay… Come here…

ALEX. Where is Mr. Paris? He said there were oysters, and—

HELEN. It matters not... Now, you know we are to go Pennsylvania, do you not?

ALEX. Yes. Why? Are we not—

HELEN. Nay, listen to me, child... Your father and I think it best that I remain in Boston.

ALEX. So we are not—

HELEN. I bid you listen Alex... I cannot make the pilgrimage to Pennsylvania, but you still may. Now, you have a choice, and you may do whatever it is you please. So do not think of me or your father. It will not pain either of us... You may go to Pennsylvania with your father, and get to spend a great deal of time with him. He'll teach you all sorts of things, and you will at last be able to see what lies beyond Boston... Or, you may stay here—with me... It is your choice...

ALEX. What will you do if—

HELEN. Do not think of me... Just do as you wish...

> (**HELEN** *turns to* **ALEXANDER,** *and the two stare at each other. For a moment,* **ALEX** *does not move— confused as to what to do. However, eventually he crosses past his mother, and goes to his father.*)

ALEX. I want to go with you—to Pennsylvania.

HELEN. *(With a weeping soul and a stoical body.)* Very well then...

ALEXANDER. I bid you go pack what you wish to bring along in a poke.

ALEX. We are to leave now?

ALEXANDER. Aye.

ALEX. Can Isom come?

ALEXANDER. No, I shall only take you. Now, bring your things.

ALEX. Yes sir...

> (**ALEX** *exits.* **HELEN** *and* **ALEXANDER** *stare at each other.*)

ALEXANDER. It is done.

HELEN. Yes. *(Beat.)* May I say goodbye to my son—alone?

ALEXANDER. You may do it in my presence—

HELEN. If he will be gone then I wish to speak to him alone! ...I beg of you.

ALEXANDER. *(He considers for a moment.)* You may... *(He begins to go out but stops. He turns to her.)* I truly loved you, Helen...

HELEN. I once loved you as well...

*(***ALEXANDER** *exits, and* **HELEN** *sits at the table. A thousand scenarios are racing through her mind.)* All will be well. All will be well... Boston will be well. Miranda will be well. Isom will be well... I will be well. I will be well... Alex— ...He— ...

> *(***ALEX** *enters and sees his mother's acute distress.)*

Will Alex be well? ...

ALEX. I will be well, mother.

HELEN. Truly?

ALEX. Truly, truly...

> *(***HELEN** *looks at* **ALEX**, *and quickly takes him into her arms. She hugs and kisses him, then relinquishes him. He looks for his father.)*

HELEN. *(Almost losing her composure.)* He's waitin' for you outside... Go on then...

ALEX. Will you be well, mother?

HELEN. Yes, I will, and when you return—all will be well.

ALEX. Truly?

HELEN. Truly, truly... I would never allow it a different way...

ALEX. *(Beat.)* Goodbye, mother.

(**HELEN** *waves silently, and* **ALEX** *exits.* **HELEN** *stares after him, unmoving, as the lights begin to fade. She turns back to the tavern doors.* **ISOM** *stands there, mute. The two stare at each other. Blackout.*)

End of Play

The Okay Kids

by

Hunter McKenzie

THE OKAY KIDS was presented in a staged reading as part of the
Thespian Playworks program at the 2015 Thespian Festival on June 27.
Phillip Moss was Director, Darren Canady served as Dramaturg, and
Samantha Allen was Stage Manager. The cast was as follows:

JACK . . . . Dalton Miller

MAX. . . . . Antonio Cipriano

ABBY . . . . .Olivia Swearingen

BARISTA . . . . Nick Brusilow

JUNE . . . . .Kiera Eriksen-McAuliffe

TINA . . . . .JeanneAnn Faris

DANNY . . . . .John Petersen

DIANNE. . . . . Grace Andreasen

OKAY KIDS . . . . Adrienne Lee, Auston Dortch,
Hannah Rabatin, Jackson Wujek

The play was first staged as part of the Winnacunnet High School
10-Minute Play Festival in 2014, co-directed by Courtney Janvrin and
Owen Thomas. The cast was as follows:

JACK . . . . .Owen Thomas

MAX. . . . . Ty Plaza

ABBY . . . . .Katrin Tharp

BARISTA . . . . Jonathan Aslin

JUNE . . . . Sara Schwab

TINA . . . . Nicki Hayden

DANNY . . . . .TJ Mason

DIANNE. . . . . .Stacie Hanson

ABOUT THE PLAYWRIGHT

Hunter McKenzie was born and raised on the seacoast of New
Hampshire, and has been writing since he was six years old. This is his
first play. He would like to thank his family, friends and specifically Kit
Rodgers and Peter Thomes for opening up the beautiful world of theatre
to him. Thanks to Darren Canady and Phillip Moss for their wonderful
guidance, kindness and for helping the play become what it is today.
Hunter currently lives in Chicago, studying Film at Columbia College.

CHARACTERS

JACK – Seventeen, male. Withdrawn, kind, and geeky.

MAX – Seventeen, male. Confident, handsome, and equally geeky.

JUNE – Seventeen, female. Enigmatic, vibrant, and down-to-earth.

ABBY – Eighteen, female. Self-assured, commanding, and conniving.

TINA – Eighteen, female. Poised, observant.

DANNY – Eighteen, male. Flirtatious, forward.

DIANNE – Seventeen, female. Ditzy, caring.

BARISTA – Sixteen, male. Awkward, obvious.

SETTING

Fictitious town of Pine Lake.

TIME

Now.

AUTHOR'S NOTES

This play is about identity. Each character is, in some way, putting on a show and not revealing his or her "true" self. Every character should have a persona put on for the world, and another real, honest one shown only for specific people (if that). The lines should move quickly in most places—except for moments that are more intimate or painful because characters aren't dancing around the truth.

This is my first play. I would like to thank my family, friends, and specifically Kit Rodgers and Peter Thomes for opening up the beautiful world of theatre to myte. Thanks also to Darren Canady and Phillip Moss for their wonderful guidance and mentorship and for helping this play become what it is today.

– Hunter McKenzie

Scene One

(Lights up on a small, cute coffee shop, with a couple of tables where people sit and sip coffee and talk. Two teenage boys enter together. It is important that they're not flamboyant.)

JACK. Five dollars is not that much. And even if it is, it wasn't a waste. It's a good movie.

MAX. No way.

JACK. *The Graduate* is a classic, Max.

MAX. It's overrated.

JACK. You're such a cynic for a good romantic movie.

MAX. Not true!

JACK. Romantic movies do have some cinematic value, dude.

MAX. Right. Says the guy who roots for Dustin Hoffman.

JACK. Max, it's not weird to root for him. He's the main character.

MAX. He was whiny. Graduates from college, debt free, and is sad because he "doesn't know what to do with his life"?!

Get a grip.

JACK. *(Mockingly, condescending.)* Like there are bigger problems in the world?

MAX. Exactly.

JACK. So what, you're a Mrs. Robinson fan?

MAX. Easily. She clearly had the better problem in the situation.

JACK. The better problem. Like it exists. Only idiots value people's problems.

MAX. Whatever. The Rialto has screened better selections. You getting coffee?

JACK. Not sure. I think I'll wait.

MAX. For who?

JACK. I'm meeting Abby here.

MAX. Oh…

>(*Quiet for a moment.*)

So am I leaving…?

JACK. You can get coffee, if you want?

MAX. Uh, nah, it's alright. I have to set up for tonight anyway.

JACK. Oh. Okay…

MAX. Well. I'll see you.

JACK. Yup.

>(**MAX** *exits where he entered, leaving* **JACK.** *He looks around for a moment. He sits at an empty table. Then, his phone rings. He answers.*)

Hey. (*A beat, listening.*) Yeah, I'm here. Waiting for you. (*Beat.*) Well, I just got here. Sorry. (*Beat.*) Okay, I'll order your coffee. (*Beat.*) Alright. I'll see you in a sec.

>(*He hangs up. After a moment, a teenage girl enters. She is* **ABBY,** **JACK**'s *girlfriend. She stands tall, confident, powerful, and commanding. She has her hair back in a tight ponytail. She's well put together, scrubbed clean. We get the feeling that she's a ranter, and he's a listener.*)

ABBY. Hi.

JACK. Hey. Sorry.

ABBY. Why are you apologizing?

JACK. I don't know. Sorry.

ABBY. Okay… (*She sits, throws down her purse and sighs.*)

JACK. What's wrong?

>(*She says nothing.*)

Abby?

(She looks at him for a moment.)

ABBY. I just don't understand why she had to be so rude when it came down to it. I mean, it's not like she's any good, you know?

JACK. Who?

ABBY. Hannah!

JACK. Oh.

ABBY. I don't know why I deal with her, she's a terrible writer.

JACK. *(Quiet, nervous.)* I think she writes well.

ABBY. Oh, please. It's contrived and unrealistic. I have to pull her back to planet Earth with each paragraph she sends me.

JACK. Well, maybe she was trying to be honest. Trying to be real, write what she knew.

ABBY. But it came off so assured and arrogant, you know? Like she was better than me. It came off so snotty.

JACK. I'm sure that wasn't it.

ABBY. Well you weren't there.

(Silence. He flinches from that little stab.)

JACK. *(Backtracking.)* You're right. I wasn't.

(Awkward silence. But she obviously can't feel that tension.)

ABBY. I mean, all I'm saying is how can I be productive and write this chapter when all I'm getting is her hot breath on my back and criticizing every letter I put on the page?

JACK. Yeah.

ABBY. It's not like she's any good! The only reason we're both in this is because of her father's connections to Harper.

JACK. Harper?

ABBY. Collins. I needed some way to get this thing published, and I thought maybe if I let her on board to do a couple of write-ups and a foreword, I would be on my way to being a published novelist.

JACK. ...That's a little devious, don't you think?

ABBY. *(Shrugging.)* The way I see it, she makes out in the end, too.

JACK. Whatever you say.

ABBY. I just didn't plan for her to be such a pain.

JACK. *(Trying to not set her off.)* I'm sure she just wants the best out of you. Tough love, you know?

ABBY. *(Venomous, almost to herself.)* Yeah, well what would you know about love?

> *(He's quiet. Looks away. She gives him a burning look, waiting for him to say something. And then:)*

I'm getting coffee.

> *(She starts to get up, when* JACK *speaks up.)*

JACK. Abby, wait—

ABBY. You know what. Whatever. This won't even take long. Listen. *(She sits down and focuses on him. Tries to be a hundred percent there.)* I've been thinking a lot lately. We need to talk.

> *(He closes his mouth, letting her talk. This happens a lot.)*

I just can't do this anymore.

> *(Silence.)*

It's just exhausting. You know? I can't do it. I'm too tired.

JACK. Do what?

ABBY. This! What this is. I...this started out fun. You know, fourth period off...have some fun in the back of your car before AP Bio...it was nice to blow off some steam with you. But then it just—

JACK. Are you breaking up with me?

ABBY. *(Grabs his hand.)* Look, it's been fun. But...you're not, this isn't... This isn't a relationship, Jack. I tried to make it one. But…you don't want one. This…us… it's just me talking and you listening. I need a guy—a man—who will have a real, intellectual conversation with me.

(Shocked silence for a moment.)

JACK. Is this a joke?

ABBY. I knew you'd be mad.

JACK. Are you kidding me?

ABBY. Look, I'm not even interested in having anything with anyone right now. With Yale in the fall—

JACK. (Angry, stammering.) Yes. I get it. We get it. We all get it—you're going to goddamn Yale, you're going to Yale in the fall!

ABBY. You're mad.

JACK. In a coffee shop?! You're doing this in a coffee shop, Abby!

ABBY. I need to focus on my book, Jack. Hannah is on a raging power trip and we need to finish before our deadline pops up. Again.

JACK. You are so self-involved.

ABBY. I'm a feminist, thank you very much!

JACK. You don't even know what that means.

ABBY. Excuse me?

JACK. You're a bitch, Abby.

(People start to look at them.)

ABBY. (Embarrassed and shocked at his crudeness.) I don't need to sit here and do this right now! I could've easily done this somewhere else.

JACK. Literally anywhere else would've been more ideal.

ABBY. (Trying to muster up kind words.) Do you know how hard this is for me? You're a nice guy. And you're smart and very talented and I only want what's best for you.

JACK. Don't patronize me.

ABBY. (Sighing.) I have to go.

JACK. I hate you. And I hate how you write. It's exactly like how you treat other people: condescending. I hate you and I hope Hannah takes creative control of your stupid self-published novel and I hope it cripples your self-importance and I hate you.

(**ABBY** *just looks at him. Smiles faintly. At this point, the entire shop is looking at them, listening.*)

ABBY. *(Hurt, sincere.)* I might be a little…harsh, Jack, but it's because I'm honest. I didn't mean to hurt your feelings. You don't have to be an asshole to prove yourself. You don't have to try to be anything.

JACK. Your book sucks.

ABBY. I tried to keep it civil… Screw you.

(She picks up her bag and exits. He sits there, stunned. Everyone else looks at him, whispers and murmurs to each other, and goes back to their own conversations. He shifts in his chair, unaware of what to do, when he pulls out his phone. He dials numbers frantically, before holding it up to his ear. He's fuming. He waits a few moments before we assume someone on the other end of the line answers.)

JACK. Max. She… I can't even believe I'm saying this but… Abby dumped me! *(Beat.)* And I'm sitting in a coffee shop where everyone is staring at me, pitying me because I just got dumped in a coffee shop! Where are you? *(Beat.)* I'm coming over. *(Beat.)* Oh come on! You have plenty of time to get ready for your party. *(Beat.)* Am I even invited to this thing?! *(Longer beat.)* Well, I am coming to it. Much to your obvious disdain. *(Beat.)* So I can't come over? *(Longest beat. Cold.)* I'll see you tonight.

(**JACK** *hangs up angrily and slams his phone down on the table. He sighs, stands, and gets in line for coffee. Moments before, a girl has entered and approached the counter. She's pretty. She's innocent-looking, almost angelic in her appearance.* **JACK** *peers at her, eyes her up and down. Does he know her? She gets to the front of the line after a moment and the* **BARISTA** *looks at her, and his eyes light up with interest.)*

BARISTA. Hi! How can I help you? Can I get you anything to drink?

JUNE. Hi, no thank you. I was just wondering if I could get an application for a job? If you guys are hiring?

BARISTA. Oh, yes! Yes, of course. We're always hiring.

JUNE. Great.

BARISTA. *(Obviously flirting with her in a clumsy way.)* You know, it's a coffee shop, it's always slow here. No one wants to work at a smelly coffee shop!

JUNE. *(Trying to humor him.)* Right.

> *(The* **BARISTA** *laughs too loud, nods too much, and stares at her breasts. Awkward.)*

So, the application?

BARISTA. Right! Right.

> *(He reaches under the counter, pulls out a stack of papers, and hands her one.)*

JUNE. Great thank you!

BARISTA. Are you sure you don't want any coffee? A bagel? We make great bagels.

JUNE. I know, but I'm fine, thank you. This is it.

BARISTA. Alriiight, but—hey. Wait a minute… Do I know you?

JUNE. *(Immediately becoming uncomfortable.)* Oh—

BARISTA. Yeah! I know you! June?! June Roberts!

JUNE. *(Smiles.)* Hi, Barry.

BARISTA. How are you?! Man, I haven't seen you since John's New Year's Eve party!

JUNE. *(With forced and unsuccessful warmth.)* Yeah.

BARISTA. It's nice to see you again! What've you been up to?!

(A **MAN** *behind* **JACK** *speaks up to the* **BARISTA***.)*

MAN. Come on, I'm in a hurry, man!

BARISTA. *(Flashing the customer a venomous look.)* Right, well—

JUNE. It's nice to see you again.

(She smiles at him. And immediately walks away towards the tables. He watches her go. While this is happening, **JACK** *realizes who the girl is. He knows the name. We see it on his face. He's watching her, too, when—.)*

BARISTA. What can I get you.

*(***JACK** *brings his attention back to the counter.)*

JACK. Can I get a refill?

(The **BARISTA** *takes his cup without a word.* **JACK** *looks back at* **JUNE***. He hesitates, then walks over to her. She sits and reads a newspaper left behind at one table. He nervously taps her shoulder.)*

June?

(She spins around in her seat, and immediately smiles. She stands up and hugs him.)

JUNE. Jack! Jack Matthews. How the hell are you?!

(He is stunned to see her.)

JACK. I'm, I'm great! How are you?

JUNE. I'm fine. I'm doing really good. Sit down!

(He sits.)

How are you? What have you been doing? How's school without me?

JACK. It's good. I'm good. I've been… I don't know, doing my thing. I…it's so nice to see you!

(The **BARISTA** *sets* **JACK***'s coffee down on the table and gives him a death glare.)*

JUNE. That's great. I'm sure Pine Lake was lost without me.

JACK. Yeah, we all miss you at school, June.

(She nods and smiles.)

So...are you back? For good?

JUNE. What do you mean?

JACK. Well...my Mom never told me that you're back, and our parents are close and I know that you, um, got, uh, sent away, at least, uh—that's what I heard from Johnny and then I heard it was a youth prison or something. I don't know. And then Kelly says she saw you over break and then everyone was talking again but you had been gone for a few months at the time...

> *(During his long, awkward and stumbling response, JUNE begins to take off her pastel cardigan. It reveals a black, ripped T-shirt with some obscure band on the chest. She lets her hair down into long, wild locks. She takes heavy jewelry out of her purse and slips it on. She finds lipstick and a miniature makeup mirror and begins to apply it, a dark shade of red. She half-listens to JACK, who as his monologue rambles on, becomes more distracted by her complete transformation.)*

...And... I was told that you had snuck out too many times or something when you were here and your parents got mad...or something... I don't know if that's—

JUNE. *(Snapping makeup tray closed.)* Okay, first of all, don't believe a word that Kelly Anderson says. She's a gossip and an Adderall addict and we both should know that by now. Second, let me get this straight: I am not the kind of girl who gets sent to reform school for "sneaking out too many times."

JACK. Oh...what's with the—?

> *(He points to her clothes, now that she's gone from sorority rush to backstage pass.)*

JUNE. Oh, right. My mom thinks a job would be good for me and wanted me to look half-presentable. And let's be real, I'd never get a real job if anyone recognized me.

JACK. Oh. Okay. I was gonna say, you looked completely different than—

JUNE. Yeah. But it's different now. Or I hope, at least.

> (*Silence for a moment.*)

Well, I should skidaddle. I've got people to see and things to do and minds to blow. (*She starts to stand and gather her things.*)

JACK. Wait! Um…

> (*She waits for him to say something. He doesn't even know exactly what he's saying.*)

Do you want to come to a party tonight?

JUNE. A June Roberts Welcome Home party?

JACK. Oh…oh, no it's not a huge—

JUNE. Kidding. Obviously. Yeah, I'll come. I assume it's Max Conner's party, right?

JACK. Yeah? How'd you know?

JUNE. I heard about it earlier when I saw an old flame at the grocery store.

JACK. Oh…cool.

JUNE. How is Max?

JACK. He's fine.

JUNE. Still movie geeky?

JACK. I guess, yeah.

JUNE. You still go to the old Rialto to watch movies all the time?

JACK. Sometimes. Not as much.

JUNE. Aw, why not? You two were my favorite bromance.

JACK. (*Uncomfortable.*) I don't know. We just don't do it that much anymore.

JUNE. Do you miss it?

JACK. I don't know, I guess. I can watch movies by myself.

JUNE. Uh huh.

JACK. We went to one today. First one in a while.

JUNE. Fun. You should tell him you want to more.

JACK. Yeah, maybe I will.

JUNE. Cool. Well, I guess I'll see ya tonight, Jacky.

JACK. *(Starstruck—***JUNE ROBERTS** *just gave him a pet name.)* Yeah, I'll see you there! Bye!

> *(By this point, she's picked up her bag and exits.* **JACK** *sits there, sort of stunned.)*

BARISTA. Dude! Your coffee!

Scene Two

(Lights up on the living room of **MAX***'s home.* **JACK**
is setting up a table of drinks, while **MAX** *sweeps
the floor obsessively.)*

JACK. And she just sat there with this smirk on her face,
like she was so much better than me! Like she knew
everything and I was some…toddler without the first
clue about the world.

MAX. *(Sweeping.)* Mhm.

JACK. And it's not like I wasn't gonna eventually break up
with her! I mean she was rude and dominating and
condescending and she had little to no appeal. But the
fact that she dumped me?! In a coffee shop! Like how
condescending can you get before you dump someone
in a hipster café with the excuse of your "novel" taking
up too much of your time?

MAX. *(Half there.)* Yeah, you're right.

JACK. And not to mention how ridiculous it is that she's
writing a book at eighteen?! And her whole psychotic
plan to get it published just shows how self-centered
and crazy she is.

MAX. Mhm.

JACK. Can you listen to me for one second?

MAX. I'm sorry! I've never had a house party before, I want
the house clean.

JACK. Max, no one's going to judge you if you're silverware
isn't polished, they're here for beer.

MAX. Whatever. I told you not to come over anyway!

JACK. And I told you I'd help set up!

MAX. But I don't need your help.

JACK. Well, I need yours!

MAX. *(Stops sweeping.)* Jack… I told you I don't want to do
that anymore.

JACK. *(Making a face.)* No! Not that. I mean with Abby, man!

(**MAX** *gives him a skeptical look.*)

Seriously! I'm serious…we don't have to—I know we don't do that anymore. We're done with that.

(**MAX** *looks at him, before going back to tidying the living room.*)

So who's even coming tonight?

MAX. People. Haley and that crowd. Jenna, Dean… Drew's bringing some of her theatre friends.

JACK. A mixed-clique party? Should be interesting.

MAX. Cam's bringing beer and I think Ali has some of the harder stuff with her.

(**JACK** *just nods. There's a brief moment of silence in the room.*)

JACK. When were you gonna invite me?

(*Another beat.*)

MAX. I didn't think you needed a formal invitation.

JACK. Why are you being like this?

MAX. Like what!

JACK. Max, I said that it was over. Why are you still punishing me?

MAX. I'm not!

JACK. My girlfriend just broke up with me and if I remember correctly, you haven't offered any condolences?

MAX. You don't need any.

JACK. What?

MAX. It's not like you liked her anyway.

JACK. And what? I liked you?

(**MAX** *looks at him.*)

MAX. I didn't say that.

JACK. But you meant it.

MAX. Well, if it weren't for Tina, would there have been an Abby?

JACK. Whatever.

> *(They go back to decorating. It's quiet for a few moments. **JACK** remembers **JUNE**'s advice.)*

We should see movies more. Like old times.

MAX. *(Annoyed or weirded out by that comment.)* Alright… whatever.

> *(Another painful quiet moment.)*

JACK. You know who I saw today?

> *(**MAX** doesn't respond.)*

Max?

MAX. Who.

JACK. June Roberts.

> *(**MAX** looks up at him, finally showing some interest.)*

MAX. June Roberts?! How? Why? When?

JACK. I don't know, she was, like, getting coffee! She was just there at the coffee shop! She was applying for a job, or something.

MAX. Does that mean she's home? Like for good?!

JACK. I guess so.

MAX. Where even was she? I heard she was at a mental hospital.

JACK. I think it was reform school.

MAX. How does she look?

JACK. Well, at first she looked like she really got it together. She had this conservative, scrubbed-clean thing going on. I almost thought she'd changed, but as soon as we started talking and the guy hiring her turns around, she's putting on red lipstick and let her hair down.

MAX. *(Scoffs.)* Sounds like June. Always playing games.

JACK. I wanted to ask her how it was at boot camp or wherever, but I never got the chance.

MAX. God, how long has she been gone?

JACK. Like…since February.

> *(They let it simmer.)*

MAX. Kinda sad. It felt like years. I was just getting used to her being gone.

> *(They ponder in silence, until—.)*

JACK. Oh! I invited her to come tonight.

MAX. Jack, I barely know her.

JACK. Max, half the people coming you barely know. Besides, if she's there, people will show up.

MAX. That's true... I don't know. It'll just be weird seeing June Roberts for the first time in forever.

JACK. Yeah...it was for me.

> *(Silence.)*

Look, I'm sorry.

MAX. Whatever. It's fine.

> *(They work a bit longer without speaking until the transition to...)*

Scene Three

> *(The same setting as before, **MAX**'s living room— except now it is filled with teenagers. A party is in low-key swing. Everyone has a red solo cup. Party music plays softly in the background. Some people stand, some people chat, some people sit on couches, some people dance. **JACK** stands alone, drinking something and watching **MAX** talk to some girl. **JACK** takes a gulp of his drink before approaching the two, who are laughing and flirting.)*

JACK. *(A little buzzed.)* Hi, Tiiinaa.

TINA. Oh, hey, Jack. How are you?

JACK. *(Sincere.)* Oh, I'm great. I'm just great. I've been at this party for an hour and a half now and I'm tipsy as hell.

MAX. You were always a lightweight.

JACK. Why do people keep labelling me as these things? Why can't I just be label-free? I'm not a canned good.

MAX. *(Starting to take away **JACK**'s cup.)* I would slow down.

JACK. *(Ignoring him, keeping the cup.)* Tina, I hear you got the female lead in Who's Afraid of Virigina Woolf?

TINA. Um, yeah, it's… I don't know, whatever. It's not a big deal.

JACK. No it's cool! Show that off!

> *(He laughs too loud.)*

TINA. *(Uncomfortable.)* Yeah.

MAX. *(Trying to get him away.)* What are you up to tonight?

JACK. *(With a fake "I don't know!" face, mocking **MAX** and pointing to his own cup.)* Probably this! Who knows?! This is really really really good music, did you pick this, Tina?

TINA. Uh, no?

JACK. *(To **MAX**.)* Why are you hitting on Tina? Like no offense Tina, you're really pretty, but she's just so… safe.

MAX. What are you talking about?

JACK. She's not gonna be as fun as meee!

MAX. Shut up, Jack.

JACK. What, all I'm saying—

MAX. *(Firm and angry).* I'll see you later, Jack.

JACK. Alright, alright. I'll go. I can take a hint. Goodbye, Maxwell. Always a pleasure, Tina.

TINA. 'Bye.

> *(**JACK** clumsily walks away, and **TINA** just looks at **MAX** questioningly. **MAX** looks concerned for his friend, but annoyed. **JACK** looks around and finds his way to the drinks table. At this moment, **JUNE** enters, taking in her surroundings. She looks a little out of place. She looks fantastic—maybe a fur coat, black jeans, and a plain white t shirt, an outfit unlike any other at the party. Her hair is unbrushed, just swept to one shoulder. She takes a seat on the couch. She sits properly, very uncomfortable, fidgeting until she sees **JACK** at the drinks table. As she approaches, he is unaware of her presence.)*

JUNE. Hey there.

JACK. *(Surprised.)* Hey! I didn't see you come in!

JUNE. You smell like Captain Morgan. Wanna leave?

JACK. *(Surprised again.)* Um…yes? Yes, yes I do.

JUNE. Great. Let's go.

> *(She grabs his hand and makes a beeline for the exit before who else but **ABBY** grabs **JACK** and pulls him back, losing **JUNE**.)*

JACK. Abby?

ABBY. Hello, Jack.

JACK. What do you want?

ABBY. Just wanted to talk to you.

JACK. Are you drunk, Abby?

ABBY. Does it matter? You look very nice tonight.

JACK. Thanks. So did ya just get here?

ABBY. I did.

JACK. So who's your date?

ABBY. Excuse me?

JACK. I'm sure you brought a date.

ABBY. What makes you think that?

JACK. *(Mean.)* You're Abby.

ABBY. I don't appreciate that comment, Jack.

JACK. Life sucks, Abby.

ABBY. For your information, I do have a date tonight. He's nice and polite and actually talks to me.

JACK. Yeah of course he does.

ABBY. It's Elijah.

JACK. Elijah? Elijah Russell.

ABBY. Yes. Elijah Russell. He didn't have practice tonight, and he asked me out.

JACK. Cute.

ABBY. *(Suggestive.)* Yeah, he is… I'm glad we have the same feelings about his looks.

> *(She looks at him. Knowingly. He looks up at her.)*

JACK. Fuck you.

> *(Silence for a moment.)*

ABBY. I know what you were doing with him. The whole time. And I had the courtesy to not mention it in the break up. So, fuck you.

> *(**JACK** has no words, stunned. And then—Splash! **ABBY** throws her drink on **JACK**'s chest. He gasps. She slips into the crowd. **JACK** just stands there. People around him notice. Especially **MAX**. Embarrassed, **JACK** storms off stage, brushing by **MAX**, who follows him. **JUNE** watches all of this happen, and as she is about to follow **JACK** and **MAX**, a girl grabs her arm.)*

DIANNE. June! Is that really you?

JUNE. Dianne! How are you?

    (We get the sense that they know each other, but are not friends enough to embrace.)

DIANNE. *(Ditzy.)* I'm—I'm great! So, I heard you went to alcohol school? How was it?!

JUNE. Oh, uh, no, that's not what it was. But it was fine.

DIANNE. Oh! Where were you, then?

JUNE. Just at this…school. It's for girls who need to kick their mischievous tendencies.

DIANNE. *(Not really getting it.)* Ooooh, cool! Did you like it?

JUNE. At first, not really. Come to think of it, I don't think I liked it much at all. But I learned a lot.

DIANNE. Oh, like what?

JUNE. Like how to run a successful Tampax smuggling ring without resorting to violence.

    (A tall and attractive boy grabs DIANNE*'s arm.)*

DANNY. June?! June, is that you!

JUNE. *(Startled to see him.)* Oh…hi Danny!

DANNY. How are you? I heard you went to some like AA school?

JUNE. Yeah, I'm good. Um, no, that's, um, not it—

DIANNE. It was a mischief school, sweetie!

DANNY. So you're just back? Like for good?

JUNE. Yep. For senior year, you know. At least, I think.

DANNY. So, what are you up to? Are you seeing anyone or…?

    (He's hitting on her. DIANNE *doesn't notice. We get the feeling this happens a lot.)*

JUNE. *(Hesitating, increasingly uncomfortable.)* Um, well, no, not particularly but… I don't know, I just don't really know if I—are you guys dating?

DIANNE. Officially together for three weeks!

DANNY. Yeah, we're, uh, going to prom together. You remember Dianne, right?

JUNE. *(Nods, holding back anger.)* Yes. We've been in the same classes since the third grade. I remember Dianne, Danny.

DANNY. So how was alcohol school?

JUNE. *(Sarcastically upbeat.)* It was peachy, Danny. Alcohol school was great. I will see you guys later.

> *(She pats **DIANNE**'s arm as she walks away, towards the drinks table. There, she looks at the alcohol and shakes her head. Just then, we hear **JACK** and **MAX** loudly arguing offstage.)*

JACK. *(Offstage.)* I don't need this right now!

MAX. *(Offstage.)* I don't care, this is my house and my business! So start talking!

> *(They enter, and the rest of the party falls silent. The two boys begin to scream at each other.)*

JACK. Well not everything is about you!

MAX. Oh, don't turn this on me!

JACK. You're so self-centered. You can't get everything you want just because you want it, Max!

MAX. What did she say to you? Was it about us?

JACK. Oh, paranoid much?

MAX. Well forgive me for being that way. You're only completely obsessed with me!

> *(Dead silence. Breathing heavy, without breaking eye contact, the two suddenly notice that the entire party is watching them. Finally **MAX**, flustered, breaks.)*

Everyone get the hell out.

DANNY. What?

MAX. Just get out!

> *(After a moment, everyone awkwardly gathers their things and makes their way to the exit, even **JUNE**. Left alone in the crippling silence, **MAX** and **JACK** still stand tall and angry at each other.)*

I want to know what you and Abby were talking about. Something about "you and him." Was that about me?

JACK. I want to know what made you such an ass.

MAX. Tell me.

JACK. Max—

MAX. Just tell me, Jack.

JACK. *(Suddenly vulnerable.)* When did you become so ashamed of me?

MAX. We were always a secret. Nothing's changed. Now, was it about—

JACK. YES! Yes. Damn it, yes it was about you. She knew. She knows. I don't know how, but that's Abby! She just knows things. She's a sneaky, conniving little—

MAX. I hope you know that I will never forgive you.

JACK. What?

MAX. You broke our deal.

JACK. I didn't—

MAX. That time in my life was supposed to be a secret and stay a secret. I don't care that you didn't tell her, she knows. She found out somehow. Our deal was to keep it a secret. You broke it.

JACK. *(Angry.)* I don't feel bad. You took a chance when you started sleeping with me. We both knew that. And you can deny it all you want, but I know that you felt something, too.

MAX. No. I didn't.

JACK. Yes you did.

MAX. No. I don't love you.

JACK. *(Half-sober.)* Come on…you can't tell me you don't remember all of our times…the night we watched Diner on your couch and—

MAX. *(Trying to hurt him more.)* I know you were more into it than me, but…jeez, I never thought you were this deep. I'm sorry for doing that. But nothing else. Because we had a deal.

JACK. Not even the first time you kissed me?

*(In all of this, **MAX** still sounds unconvincing. There is something there between them. **MAX** recognizes how hurt **JACK** is.)*

MAX. *(Cold.)* I'm sorry I couldn't be what you wanted.

JACK. *(Drunk and sloppy and honest.)* You were what I wanted. You were all I wanted. And I never wanted Abby! I never wanted you to be with Tina! I just wanted you! I didn't need you to be anything or anyone! I just wish you could've been…better. I wish every time you looked at me it wasn't with disgust… I wish I could've been enough.

MAX. *(Forced.)* Well, you weren't.

JACK. You slept with me for four months. We were friends long before then. We did some pretty intense things—

MAX. And how, exactly, are we supposed to come back from that, from what we did? How are we supposed to go back to simple friendship? And do you know how exhausting it is to be your friend?

*(That hits. **JACK** just looks at him with hurt. There is a long, painful moment where neither says anything. But then **JACK** stands and quietly moves to **MAX**, hugs him from behind. At first, **MAX** fights it—then surrenders. It is their first moment of physical intimacy that the audience can see. It is important and raw.)*

JACK. *(Breaking away.)* Thanks for inviting me tonight.

*(He quietly exits. **MAX** says nothing. He looks around at his trashed house.)*

Scene Four

(Lights up on empty stage. The only thing that is on the stage are two matching lawn chairs. We are outside of **MAX**'s *house. One of the lawn chairs is occupied by* **JUNE**. **JACK** *walks in, visibly upset. The two notice each other at the same time.)*

JUNE. Are you okay?

JACK. Fine. *(He keeps walking past her.)*

JUNE. *(Jumping up.)* Hey! Wait!

JACK. *(Stopping and turning.)* What?

JUNE. I just…come sit.

(He hesitates.)

Come on.

(JACK *finally plops down next to her. Stiff and sad.)*

It's so quiet. I miss that.

(We hear sounds of crickets in the night. It's peaceful.)

That was easily the worst party I've ever been to.

JACK. Agreed.

JUNE. How many parties have you gone to?

JACK. Touché.

JUNE. I can't believe that party even got you drunk.

JACK. I'm not drunk.

JUNE. Right, Mr. I Reek of Liquor.

JACK. Whatever. It's freezing out here, I have to go home.

JUNE. Wait! Just…stay. What happened to you and Max?

JACK. Nothing. It's fine.

JUNE. You sure?

JACK. Yes. And what are you doing out here?

JUNE. I just needed some peace and quiet.

(They sit there in silence.)

JACK. Where did you go to school for all that time, June?

JUNE. "Hollow Hills School for the Troubled Youth," New York.

JACK. Wow.

JUNE. Hardcore, right?

> (*They don't say anything. She goes into her purse.*)

Where are my keys?

JACK. Hm?

JUNE. Huh, I can't seem to find my keys.

JACK. Are they not in there?

JUNE. I don't think so…where are they! (*At first, she's pretty calm about it. She digs in her bag and gets more frustrated. She dumps out her purse on her lap, and looks through it.*)

Where are my goddamn keys!

JACK. Hey—

JUNE. Where the hell are they?! (*She shoves all of her belongings on the ground and springs up.*) I think I might've left them inside.

JACK. Hey, we can find them later, it's not—

JUNE. I need my goddamn keys! Where the hell could they have gone?!

JACK. (*Standing up.*) I don't know, we'll find—

JUNE. I NEED THEM NOW, JACK! WHERE ARE MY KEYS?!

JACK. HEY—calm down?! We'll find them.

> (*She stops, taking a deep breath. He looks at her, and then looks at her mess on the ground. He kneels down.*)

They're right here, June. They were in your bag.

JUNE. (*Relieved and self-conscious.*) Well, thank God. Sorry.

> (*She kneels down next to him and takes them.*)

JACK. Why was that such a big deal?

> (*She says nothing. She stares at her keys.*)

What's wrong?

> (**JUNE** *tries to say something, takes a breath. And then her face crumples. She starts crying.* **JACK** *is surprised and uncomfortable.*)

Hey…hey, it's okay. Don't worry. We found them. I didn't mean to yell.

> (*She cries more.*)

What's wrong?

> (*She stands up, shoving things into her purse, and starts to leave.*)

June!

JUNE. (*Spins around.*) NOTHING IS WRONG! Leave me alone!

> (**JACK** *says nothing. She crumples again.*)

JACK. Is it me or did this just go from 0 to 100 in like five seconds? Why do you need your keys?

JUNE. I can't do this.

JACK. Do what?!

JUNE. (*Rambling, anxious, loud.*) I just don't know what's wrong and why I'm not happy to be home and I hated Hollow Hills but it seems better and better each passing second I spend in this hellhole and I hate Danny and Dianne and everyone here. I don't know where I'm going to be happy or if I will be at all, and it feels like an elephant is sitting on my chest.

> (*She stands there for a moment, crying, and then walks over to him and hugs him, searching for comfort.* **JACK** *is too confused and shocked to resist, and slowly hugs back.*)

JACK. I'm sorry.

JUNE. It's fine, I just have this…nervous thing that sometimes spikes out of control. The Hills tried to help me kick that, but I guess it wasn't so successful.

> *(She calms down for a second, and slowly looks up at* **JACK.** *They make eye contact. And then she kisses him. For a good, long moment. And then she breaks it.* **JACK** *is dumbfounded. There was no spark.)*

I'm sorry.

JACK. No, don't apologize. It's fine.

JUNE. I'm really sorry.

JACK. I said you didn't have to apologize.

> *(Silence.)*

(Trying to break the tension, playful.) Now stop hitting on me, okay!

> *(They both laugh a little. He sits next to her.)*

JUNE. I never asked you, why are you covered in rum?

JACK. Oh, well, I got the wonderful privilege of having a raging bitch throw her drink on me.

JUNE. First tip, don't ever call a girl that. Everyone's got their own stuff, you know? You don't have to single her out because she has a vagina.

JACK. Sorry.

JUNE. So who's this girl? Why'd she feel the need to throw alcohol all over your nice shirt?

JACK. Abby Patterson. We broke up earlier today, and…it wasn't pretty.

JUNE. You and Abby dated? No way! Abby was in my sophomore Bio class. She was…strong-minded. Why'd you break up?

JACK. *(Hesitating.)* Um…things just…didn't work out. In the end. It wasn't love, I guess.

JUNE. You don't really believe in all of that, do you?

JACK. I don't know. I'd like to think we don't have to go through life alone.

JUNE. *(Unconvinced.)* Right. So why'd you really break up?

JACK. I think it's your turn for some questions.

JUNE. I'm an open book. Ask away.

JACK. What happened that made you have to leave?

JUNE. *(JUNE hesitates herself.)* I was caught at a party. I think I was technically arrested. My parents were livid. And it had been building to that moment, 'cuz I had done really stupid stuff before that and when they found out I was at the police station…something snapped inside them, I guess. They'd had it with me. Danny Fuller, you know Danny? He got me drunk and I guess we hooked up and he ditched me when the cops showed up. *(A beat. Then small.)* I didn't even have a bra on when the cops were barging down the door…when my parents picked me up at like, three a.m… I was stoned and piss-drunk out of my mind. So they sent me to Hollow Hills. *(She seems very, very sad. In ways we will never know.)* And now I'm back.

JACK. Jeez.

JUNE. What?

JACK. Well… You were always the girl who looked so, together. Up until like freshman year you always wore nice clothes to school, you had perfect grades, I saw you at church every time I went…

JUNE. I don't know what to tell you, people change. My parents were good at keeping me in line.

> *(They sit in quiet for a moment.)*

I guess I just…like didn't see the point in anything. I was such a cliché, I started going to more parties. Hooking up with a lot of guys. I tried to be this all-knowing intellectual who was above everyone else because I thought I had the cynical secrets to the Universe. I was literally called "Merlot Girl" for like five months because I brought my own bottle of wine to an open house rager once. I was such a snob.

JACK. You were a great mystery that no one could ever figure out.

JUNE. That was the goal. The very pretentious goal.

JACK. I guess I just don't understand.

JUNE. Understand what?

JACK. I don't understand why you have to pretend to be someone?

(She doesn't say anything for a minute.)

JUNE. I like to pretend. Real life sorta sucks and you gotta just shake things up. Going to a different school really shows you how much none of this matters. It becomes so claustrophobic and…boring. Like life's not worth living if you have to live here. That's why I'm going back to New York in the fall. You know, one of my teachers at Hollow Hills told me something once in the early months that I was there. I was sneaking out with my roommate and my English teacher had caught us off property and she sat me down after class the next day and said something I feel like I'll never forget: "You can always turn an inkblot into a butterfly." I don't know, at first I thought it was really cheesy and she probably says it to all of the kids, but it stuck with me. And it still sticks.

JACK. Do you miss Danny? As a boyfriend?

JUNE. I mean…not really. Two years of his bullshit was enough. Hollow Hills taught me to find my feminine power, if anything.

JACK. The "I don't need a man" mentality.

JUNE. It's a good one. Hollow Hills did teach me a lot.

(No one says anything for another moment.)

JACK. So why would you leave again before senior year?

JUNE. Because I hate this place.

JACK. But…why would you run away from your issues? I feel like that's not helping.

JUNE. *(Skeptical.)* So you think I should stay here for the rest of school?

JACK. In my opinion.

(Quiet.)

JUNE. Why did you break up with your girlfriend, Jack?

> (JACK *sits there and lets his fears and his sadness and quiet frustrations pile up on him.*)

JACK. When did it all get so gray and blurry and confusing? Literally everything. I don't know what I'm trying to do or trying to be. I looked at her and I felt…nothing. But when I was with Max it was different. It didn't feel… right, but it felt closer to it.

> (*Silence.*)

JUNE. You hooked up with Max, didn't you?

JACK. Embarrassing, huh?

JUNE. No. I'm all for gay rights, I just never pegged you—

JACK. (*Not entirely convincing.*) I'm not gay.

JUNE. Okay.

> (*They're quiet.*)

Do you remember when we had a class together in the third grade?

JACK. Mrs. Clark?

JUNE. Yeah.

JACK. We were friends back then, remember?

JUNE. I do…and my Mom actually pulled out all of my old school projects and stuff when I was gone. I guess she missed me or something.

JACK. Okay.

JUNE. And today after I got home from seeing you, I was going through it, and I found something. From you.

JACK. From me?

> (*She's going through her purse, and pulls out a folded, slightly crinkled red card from inside her wallet.*)

Oh, my god. I remember that.

JUNE. (*Reading card.*) "June, thank you very much for making third grade very good so far. You are a nice friend and I love you very much. Happy Valentine's Day."

(They chuckle at it. He takes it and looks at it.)

JACK. My N's are backwards in Valentine's.

(They both laugh.)

JUNE. You were my old Valentine.

JACK. The very first of many.

JUNE. (Laughing.) Shut up, Jack.

(She punches his arm. And then they sit in silence
for a couple of moments.)

JACK. If only the little me knew that his future Valentine would be the kid who helped him with his math tables.

JUNE. Max?

(JACK nods. He touches the paper card.)

He means a lot to you.

JACK. Whatever. It doesn't matter anyway. He couldn't care less about me.

JUNE. That's not true.

JACK. I just wish I could make him understand how well we'd work together.

(Silence.)

Nothing to say?

JUNE. Well…

JACK. What?

JUNE. It's nothing.

JACK. Say it.

JUNE. Well… I mean. It doesn't take a genius to know that I haven't really got any friends. At least, ones that stuck around and waited for me to come back. It's not easy to find a person as genuine and caring as Max.

JACK. And?

JUNE. And why would you risk losing him? Don't you value your friendship more than your Not-relationship relationship?

JACK. *(Thinks for a moment, a realization.)* Yeah… I do.

JUNE. I guess we both want something we can't have.

JACK. Well… I have to get going. Curfew.

JUNE. Yeah. Me too. I'd rather be home than at this party for once.

JACK. *(Chuckling.)* Yeah.

JUNE. Need a ride? The mother in me doesn't want you driving home.

JACK. Nah, it's alright. I'll walk.

JUNE. Okay.

> *(They look each other in the eyes, and slowly start to walk off in opposite directions.)*

Hey, Jack!

JACK. Yeah?

JUNE. Thank you.

> *(They stride back over to each other, meet at center and hug.)*

JACK. It's nice to have you home, June.

JUNE. It's good to be home. I think I'll stay for a while.

JACK. No New York?

JUNE. I think I'll stick around for a little bit. See if I can tough it out.

JACK. That's really good to hear.

JUNE. I'll see you around.

JACK. Bye, June.

> *(JUNE exits. JACK idly walks the stage, hands in his pockets, reflecting on the night. He finally settles in the lawn chair again, and then MAX walks on from stage left with a bag of party trash.)*

MAX. Oh, hey.

JACK. Hi.

MAX. You stuck around?

JACK. What do you mean?

MAX. You're on my front lawn.

JACK. Oh yeah. I'm really drunk. I can't go anywhere.

(**MAX** *laughs. The two hold their positions.*)

Look, Max—

MAX. I don't need it right now, Jack.

JACK. No, I—

MAX. I'm really not in the mood to argue with you again.

JACK. No, me neither. I just… I wanted to apologize.

(**MAX** *says nothing.*)

I think both of us had different expectations for whatever we were, and… I let that get in the way of us, our friendship. I didn't mean to embarrass you or—

MAX. Don't worry about it.

(*Beat.*)

I'm glad you're still here. I wanted to make sure you were good. I understand if you hate me.

JACK. You're my best friend, Max, I don't know how to hate you.

MAX. I'm just…trying to figure things out.

JACK. I know you are. So am I. I don't want to force anything.

MAX. I love you—you know that, right?

JACK. I do.

MAX. I just don't know if I love you in that way.

JACK. That's okay.

(*Quiet.*)

Can we just, not be mad anymore?

MAX. Sure.

JACK. I'll help you clean up your house.

>(**JACK** *and* **MAX** *now walk off stage together. The lights go down.*)

End of Play

It's Gonna Rain

by

Matthew Waterman

IT'S GONNA RAIN was presented in a staged reading as part of the Thespian Playworks program at the 2015 Thespian Festival on June 27. John Morris was Director, Nicholas C. Pappas served as Dramaturg, and Dacota Schwarte served as Stage Manager. The cast was as follows:

MIRA . . . . Elizabeth Miller

NISHA . . . . Julia Sismour

CHARLIE . . . . ` Duncan Weinland

EMILY . . . . Kelsey Reese

KANSA . . . . Nina Rivera

ACUERA . . . . Sam Ducharme

ABOUT THE PLAYWRIGHT

Matthew Waterman, a 2015 graduate of Bloomington (Indiana) High School North, is in the jazz studies program at Indiana University in Bloomington.

FROM THE EDITORS OF DRAMATICS MAGAZINE

It's Gonna Rain presents three teenaged couples at a crossroads in time. Nisha, Mira, Charlie, and Emily are high school seniors in southern Indiana, unsure of themselves and their relationships as college, adulthood, and other pressures loom. Their scenes alternate with episodes from the distant past, as Kansa and Acuera, seventeen-year-old female lovers from a Fort Ancient tribe, struggle with similar passions and uncertainties, under very different life circumstances.

We chose *Rain* for Playworks knowing that the mature content would challenge student actors at the Thespian Festival—a challenge they all met bravely and capably, despite some difficult moments in rehearsal. We also knew that come publication time, we were going to have more problems. The play deals very frankly with teenaged sexuality and marijuana use, and much of the language falls outside our own comfort zone as an educational magazine with a mixed-aged readership that includes many school libraries. Any attempt to make *Rain* more suitable for the classroom or school stage would, we felt, diminish the play. So, in consultation with playwright Matthew Waterman, we selected for publication in *Dramatics* (October 2015 issue) a few representative scenes that capture the central relationship between Nisha and Mira, and which could stand on their own as an acting exercise or performance piece for advanced student actors. The excerpts contain a few profanities (including the f-word, historically banned from our pages), but they struck us as PG-13-rated, compared to the more R-rated Charlie/Emily and Kansa/Acuera scenes. This acting edition presents the entire script, as Matthew Waterman wrote it, and for that we applaud Samuel French, Inc. Reader discretion is advised.

CHARACTERS

MIRA – Seventeen then eighteen, female, a student at Bloomington High School North in the year 2015

NISHA – Seventeen then eighteen, female, likewise

CHARLIE – Seventeen then eighteen, male, likewise

EMILY – Seventeen then eighteen, female, likewise

KANSA – *(KAHN-suh)*, seventeen, female, a member of the Fort Ancient people in the year 1015

ACUERA – *(uh-KWEH-ra)*, seventeen, female, likewise

The characters are all seventeen years old at the beginning of the play. Mira, Nisha, Emily and Charlie are all students at Bloomington High School North in southern Indiana, in the present day; Kansa and Acuera are both female members of the Fort Ancient tribe of people who lived in the area in prehistoric times.

SETTING

The play takes place on and around a rock in Brown County State Park (a bit east of Bloomington, a bastion of liberal sensibility in a conservative state). The modern scenes are set from August 2015 through November 2016. Kansa and Acuera's scenes take place in the same exact location a thousand years prior, but of course it is not Brown County State Park at that time. Somewhere onstage is a jagged wooden sign that reads "DO NOT SIT ON ROCK," visible for the modern scenes but perhaps masked or backlit to appear part of the natural surroundings in the prehistoric scenes.

AUTHOR'S NOTES

Sentences with exclamation points should sometimes be spoken with finality. Sentences with periods should rarely be spoken with finality. Sentences without end punctuation should not be spoken with finality. Sentences with question marks should be spoken with the opposite of finality.

Important And/Or Established Ideas Are Capitalized In This Manner (thanks David Mamet). Sum werds r spilld thuh way charikterz say thim (thanks Suzan-Lori Parks). Paragraph breaks occur when characters move on to new subtopics. Parentheses in dialogue denote (the portion of the line that is overlapped by the following one).

I recommend use of transition music and possibly underscoring. Two specific suggestions: "Intro," from 2014 Forest Hills Drive by J. Cole, and at the end of the play, "It's Gonna Rain, Part I," from the 1965 Steve Reich piece.

For Mia.

Scene One

(Play "Intro," from 2014 Forest Hills Drive *by J. Cole*. Lights up on* **KANSA** *and* **ACUERA**. *Lights of various colors fade up and down.* **KANSA** *lies in* **ACUERA***'s embrace as* **ACUERA** *pets her gently. The song ends as we fade to black.)*

---

*A license to produce *It's Gonna Rain* does not include a performance license for "Intro" by J. Cole. The publisher and author suggest that the licensee contact ASCAP or BMI to ascertain the rights holder to acquire permission for performance of this song. If permission is unattainable, the licensee should create an original composition in a similar style. For further information, please see music use note on page 3.

Scene Two

> (**NISHA** *and* **MIRA** *sit on the rock, overlooking the vast expanse of Indiana forest and scanning the gloaming sky for stars.*)

MIRA. Oh—a star!

NISHA. Yes!

MIRA. And,

> (*She points to another.*)

that one.

NISHA. Mira, do you think I could be an astronaut?

MIRA. Ehhh…

NISHA. If I *really* tried

MIRA. Sure.

NISHA. I could take pictures from the moon and send them to you.

MIRA. That would be so nice.

NISHA. Selfies.

> (*Silence.* **MIRA** *puts her hand on the very top of* **NISHA**'s *chest. Even though they could lie there forever,* **NISHA** *must speak.*)

Okay, yeah. I just need to say, now, Mira… I am—but, actually, first—okay—Can I say something? But I need to, like, look a little bit away, and you also have to promise to be—um…you have to be honest, okay??

MIRA. Yeah.

NISHA. So I feel like you should know this, but I need to make it clear—the thing was, that…okay. Well, first: It must be acknowledged, I don't think we need to… pack, or cram something in…well okay I guess that has to be the second part.

The first part is—this is hard to say the words—I am Attracted to you. And, well, it's that you're my Best Friend, and I am attracted to you Platonically, but also Romantically, and Sexually and before you say, whatever, you have to…say the absolute truth, because it's *High Stakes*. And that brings us back to what I was saying before, which is:

I know we are—it's our senior year of high school, and we will have to…choose colleges at the end of this year, and that might involve, for one or both of us, moving away. In which case, any… Romantic Relationship between us would not be… 'twould not behoove us. So if that is the case, maybe we should never start it, but all this is secondary because it doesn't matter unless it were true that the, astronomically low chance of you returning these feelings was…true.

MIRA. Nisha—

NISHA. But that's why you have to be *honest,* cause if you said, "yes," or whatever, but it wasn't true, we would be…together, and it *would not* work out. Or if you say "no," it would be okay. So you have to—

MIRA. *(Keeping it real.)* Yes.

 (Pause.)

Yeah.

NISHA. As in…

MIRA. I do too.

NISHA. Really?

MIRA. Yeah, I…endorse this.

NISHA. You aren't—

MIRA. I am quite confident in my endorsement of this.

NISHA. Okay. So… I should kiss you now? That's right, right?

MIRA. I'm pretty sure, yeah.

NISHA. Okay, so I guess we just do it.

MIRA. All right. Okay. I'm ready.

 (NISHA kisses MIRA for a moment. They crack up.)

NISHA. *(Genuine.)* Great.

 (They laugh a bit and go for another kiss.)

Scene Three

  (EMILY lies across CHARLIE's lap where NISHA and MIRA were.)

CHARLIE. Wanna get fireworks for Thanksgiving this year?

EMILY. ? … Yeah, actually thad be on fleek.

CHARLIE. We should have sex tonight.

EMILY. No, Charlie, I don't want to.

CHARLIE. Why

EMILY. I just don't want to.

CHARLIE. Ugh, I don't wanna write that fucking *Beowulf* paper.

EMILY. Turn it in late.

  (EMILY checks her phone and starts replying to a text.)

CHARLIE. Emily, why are you texting Neil Grantman?

EMILY. We're texting about D&D this weekend.

CHARLIE. Okay

EMILY. What?

CHARLIE. I just don't like you hanging out with Neil and Ryan when I'm not there.

EMILY. Okay

CHARLIE. I don't understand why you don't wanna have sex tonight

EMILY. I dunno, I just don't feel like it and I have to write that paper.

CHARLIE. *(Leaving.)* Well then let's just leave.

EMILY. Okay.

  (EMILY follows.)

Scene Four

(CHARLIE and NISHA smoke a bowl throughout the scene.)

CHARLIE. Wait, so you've been here before?

NISHA. Yeah, I have.

CHARLIE. Shit. I didn't think many people knew about this spot. Emily and I come here to have sex.

NISHA. Will you shut up?

CHARLIE. What?

NISHA. Just shut the fuck up. First of all, Emily is someone whom I consider a close friend, and for you to tell me that you boned her on a rock in Brown County State Park is not cool. And second: I don't understand why you feel the need to brag about your sex life (every time we hang out.)

CHARLIE. What, it's true. Don't be such a dick, I wouldn't …say whatever if you said you were having sex with Mira here.

NISHA. Yeah, it wouldn't come up because I would never say that.

CHARLIE. Are you?

NISHA. Jesus.

CHARLIE. *Are* you?

NISHA. *(Joke.)* Yeah, every morning at 8 a.m.

CHARLIE. *(Joke.)* Dyke.

Scene Five

(**MIRA** *and* **EMILY** *arrive at the spot.*)

MIRA. How do you know this place?

EMILY. Uh…hiking. Have you been here?

MIRA. Yeah.

EMILY. ?

MIRA. Hiking.

(*Pause.*)

EMILY. It's really pretty up here.

MIRA. Yeah.

EMILY. It's like…one of those places where you feel like you're the only people in the world when you're here, you know?

MIRA. Yeah.

EMILY. Like you could just stay here forever, and you wouldn't have to worry about school, or anything. And no one would know.

MIRA. Mmmm

(*Pause.*)

EMILY. Are you dating Nisha?

MIRA. Yeah.

EMILY. *(<3 <3 <3 <3 <3)* Good. I shipped that shit hardcore since freshman year.

MIRA. *(☺)* I shipped it too.

EMILY. Took you long enough.

MIRA. Well, it's happening now.

(*Pause.*)

So, what about, like, college?
What about it?

EMILY. Like, for you and Nisha. Are you gonna stay here and go to IU? Or, is she?

MIRA. Ummmmm…!

EMILY. What?

MIRA. I don't know!

EMILY. *(As in: "I was just asking")* Okay…!

MIRA. No, it's fine, I just…oh god, I really just don't know.

EMILY. Okay.

MIRA. What about you and Charlie?

EMILY. Yeah, we're both going to IU.

(**MIRA** *smiles and nods a bit.*)

Scene Six

(**NISHA** *and* **MIRA** *embrace each other.*)

NISHA. I love guinea pigs so much.

MIRA. They're very precious.

NISHA. Why am I not a guinea pig.

MIRA. You would get so bored!

NISHA. No I wouldn't! They mostly just sit, but they're usually thinking grand thoughts.

MIRA. Do you want to try one of your awe–inspiring monologues?

NISHA. Oh, sure.

MIRA. Okay. I'm ready.

NISHA. All right. Here's one. Okay: Okay so this is based on great Time, great distances of Time. Like Thousands of Years. Okay:

MIRA. All right.

NISHA. Do you ever imagine…

(*Thunder—a sudden distraction.*)

It's gonna rain.

MIRA. I love rain.

NISHA. Rain loves you.

MIRA. The monologue.

NISHA. Yes, about Time. All right:

Do you ever imagine what may have been occurring in any particular location…five *hundred* years ago, or A Thousand Years Ago? I think we tend to view The Earth as this thing that we are on now, as it stands, and we really only feel the weight of *our* world. You know what I mean?

(**MIRA** *nods "yes."*)

We learn about history, and we believe it's true and, it's interesting, but it remains this text in a book or in our heads and, we don't *feel* it the way that we *feel* our lives, and the things that happen with us. It doesn't permeate our emotional universes really, it stays in the realm of facts. We don't get the…sense that those people who existed hundreds of years ago were *actually real people.* That they *existed, In The Flesh* and…and they were absolutely as beautiful and complicated and grand and as…soulful as us. And they fell in love, and lost their children, and buried their children in the ground, and they had parents and loved them. Those people… there were *actual real human beings* probably where we are, right now, One Thousand Years Ago. There were probably people in this location, maybe two people who were looking at the stars, or two people who fell in love and held each other in *this* location, as real as us. Imagine *talking* to them, *connecting*…with them. Even historical people, they had all the, thoughts of us, and, all the—they did all the things we do, like… *Aristotle.* He was a *guy,* you know, he could walk right up to us and say "hey," he—I mean, he took *shits.* Imagine Aristotle takin a shit. Picture that.

MIRA. Oh, great.

NISHA. Yeah, well, okay, sorry, that's, gross, but—you get the point.

MIRA. But what's sad is no one remembers those people. The vast majority of people who've lived on Earth… like, no one has any idea about. They're just erased and completely forgotten, as if they never existed. And all their memories, which, like you said, were so complex and beautiful are just gone now. Nonexistent. And that's how ours will be. Which is sad. Because my memories feel so important.

NISHA. They are important. You're important.

MIRA. You did a good monologue.

NISHA. Well, I was…fuckin serious.

(**MIRA** *laughs. She kisses* **NISHA.**)

MIRA. And it *would* be special to connect with those two people, from a thousand years ago. Like us.

NISHA. Precisely.

> (**MIRA** *kisses* **NISHA.**)

MIRA. To witness what they—

> (**NISHA** *kisses* **MIRA.** *Then* **MIRA** *kisses* **NISHA.**)

Probably those two people made out here a long time ago.

> (*They make out. After some kissing,* **NISHA** *reaches into* **MIRA***'s shirt to her breast.*)

Scene Seven

(**CHARLIE** *and* **EMILY** *have replaced* **NISHA** *and* **MIRA***, making out on the rock. After some kissing,* **CHARLIE** *reaches into* **EMILY***'s shirt.)*

EMILY. Can you give me a ride to Neil's house tomorrow?

CHARLIE. Sure. What time?

EMILY. Like… 2.45.

CHARLIE. Do you wanna do like 2, and we can have sex before?

EMILY. Sure.

CHARLIE. Or we could just do it there.

EMILY. *(Laughing.)* Yeah, a foursome with Neil and Ryan.

CHARLIE. Hey I need to tell you about something.

EMILY. Well, do you want to tell me it with your hand on my left tit?

CHARLIE. *(Removes the hand)* …

EMILY. So what is it?

CHARLIE. So this morning, Mira walked—well I had given Lauren a ride to school and we were in my car, and, you know how she was like, really weird and into me?

EMILY. ?

CHARLIE. Well anyway she like, tried to kiss me, and Mira walked by and saw it, and I just wanted to let you know, before Mira told you, that I really was not… participating, and Lauren kissed me—

EMILY. Why would you not just stop her?

CHARLIE. I—I tried, and she just did it

EMILY. It's not that hard to stop (someone from kissing you)

CHARLIE. Well, whatever, I'm (telling you)

EMILY. I'm just trying to understand: okay, so we've been Dating for *eight months* and Lauren decides to kiss you, and you let it happen, and it's happening at *least* long enough for Mira (to see, then)

CHARLIE. It was *two seconds*, not—she just happened to be
 passing (by at that exact time)

EMILY. Ugh, I don't—ugh, god—(I don't know, what)

CHARLIE. Well, I told (you, so)

EMILY. Yeah, cuz you knew Mira would tell me (anyway)

CHARLIE. Whatever, I didn't know—

EMILY. FUCK YOU.

> (**EMILY** *grabs* **CHARLIE** *by the hair and starts
> jerking him around.*)

CHARLIE. Jesus! Fuck, get off me!

> (**CHARLIE** *struggles free and* **EMILY** *slaps him four
> times in the head. She kicks his balls.*)

Fuck! God! Fuck!

> (**CHARLIE** *fights back, elbowing* **EMILY** *in the face,
> but he doesn't stand a chance. It's brutal.* **EMILY**
> *throws him into the rock, shoves him onto the
> ground and exits.*)

Shit…oh god…oh my fucking god…

> (*After a moment,* **EMILY** *enters. She looks at*
> **CHARLIE** *on the ground. She goes and helps
> him up. She exits, leaving him behind until the
> blackout.*)

Scene Eight

*(**NISHA** and **MIRA** mount the rock.)*

NISHA. *(Sensing stress in **MIRA**'s breathing)* Are you...doin good?

MIRA. What? Yeah, I'm just...tired.

NISHA. You're tired?

MIRA. And stressed.

NISHA. Why?

MIRA. Because

NISHA. Because why.

MIRA. Because I have to decide on a school in...three days.

NISHA. Oh yeah...we, maybe, should talk (about that.)

MIRA. Nooooo(ooooooooo)

NISHA. Yeeeeeee(eeessssssssss)

MIRA. I...noooooooo(ooooooo.)

NISHA. Okay, whatever, but I just need to say: You need to do what *you* want, without regard to me. Well, okay, not without regard to how you would feel regarding me but without regard to how I would feel. That is, without regard to how I would feel with regard to how you feel with regard to me. I mean it's about what's best for you. With regard to your education.

MIRA. ...

NISHA. I'm sorry, I shouldn't...say (things that)

MIRA. No, don't be sorry! What are *you* deciding?

NISHA. I...don't know or I won't tell you unless you say.

MIRA. You don't know or you won't tell me?

NISHA. I just feel like... everyone would say, or does say it's stupid to make such a large decision with consideration for who is your romantic partner, but that runs counter to my...

I'm going to IU.

(Pause.)

MIRA. I'm sorry.

NISHA. What? Why?

    *(Pause while **MIRA** gathers courage.)*

MIRA. I don't think I'm staying here.

    (Long pause.)

NISHA. I…

Scene Nine

(KANSA and ACUERA at the spot.)

KANSA. *(Laughing.)* That's an exaggeration…

ACUERA. *(Laughing.)* I'm only tellin you that when Balda looks at you, and it's like that cold heat in her eyes: it's just a *tiny bit* worse than like, maybe getting hit in the vagina with a pick axe.

KANSA. Eloquent, Acuera.

(Laughs and a pause.)

ACUERA. Kansa, talk about—do a monologue.

KANSA. Ah. Okay. Ready?

ACUERA. Ready for Freddie.

KANSA. Okay, this one will be about…the future.

ACUERA. Okay.

KANSA. The future. As in, what could be possible in the future:

Do you ever imagine the future? There could be…anything. Two people with, like, *us* in the future? In any particular location—for example, like, this one. What if there's like two people here, talking about…like…our stuff. Thinking too. How much of time, or, from time, could the future stretch? Or how far back, or, long ago does it even stretch. Like a thousand years—imagine here or…wherever or who could…stand here in a thousand years ago. I mean: from now. Will the world have ended? Or will people be…somehow different, like, in the future?

ACUERA. Please stop this.

(They laugh a bit.)

KANSA. I'd like to see you fuckin try, Acuera.

ACUERA. Look. It doesn't necessarily have to be—just because it's about grand things doesn't mean it has to be made of…ideas. It can be made of feelings. I mean, fuck an idea, feelings are the most grand shit out there. Honestly, fuck ideas, monologues are for feelings.

KANSA. Okay hoe, let's hear a feelings monologue.

ACUERA. Wait, but: when are you supposed to be back home?

KANSA. I don't know, just…after sundown.

ACUERA. Okay, the sun is down.

KANSA. In a while.

ACUERA. Don't you need to be back on time? Don't you care what your dad thinks?

KANSA. Not really.

ACUERA. Kansa. You realize what your father thinks is the sole determinant of if we will be able to stay together.

KANSA. I care about you more than him and his fucking plans.

ACUERA. If you don't stay on his good side, he won't listen to you and you will have to (go up North.)

KANSA. He won't do it, he's just…bluffing.

ACUERA. To what end?

KANSA. To the *end* that he will *end* our relationship.

ACUERA. You mean I shouldn't start work (for Balda?)

KANSA. No, no—commit to Balda, it'll be fine.

ACUERA. I have to make this decision, I have to be a maverick here. You know there's no turnin back when you commit to working for fuckin Balda. She'll ruin your life.

KANSA. Sorry. I don't mean to make things hard for you.

ACUERA. Don't be sorry. It's not your fault.

KANSA. I know it's not my fault, I'm still sorry though.

ACUERA. There should be a word for that.

KANSA. Maybe it'll all work out. Maybe I can stay and you can…weave shit all day. Doesn't that sound amazing?

ACUERA. It does sound amazing.

KANSA. We're running out of time. Let's hear that feelings monologue that will apparently be so much fuckin better than mine.

ACUERA. Well, okay. So it's about big and grand feelings. The feelings that can swallow us up and make us feel like are lives are the size of The Universe. And these feelings, all my best and grandest feelings, are about you.

KANSA. Lay it on me.

ACUERA. All right:

So basically, sometimes, I feel like every person has someone who they connect with perfectly, unbelievably, fantastically, on the Friendship level. And you can laugh with them and do stupid shit with them and it's awesome.

Then everyone has someone who's like their perfect… Romance…person. You wanna hold them, and kiss them, and really truly make them happy. All that stuff.

Then, also, and finally, you have your ideal Sexual companion. That person who you are absolutely goddamn desperate to fuck. That hardcore primal shit, you know, where you want your face and her pussy and your mouth and her nipples to all be crammed into one infinitesimal space. Her naked body surpasses all the glory of the Earth, the Sky, the Water, and the Stars, and you yearn to behold that glory for all eternity.

Everyone has these three people at some point in their life. But…what happens when these three people—the person you most wanna joke around with, the person you most wanna hold in your arms, and the person you most wanna have sex with—what happens when they're all the same person?

What I'm saying is…that's kind of you, Kansa. You are those people for me. All three of them.

KANSA. Wow

(Play "Intro," from 2014 Forest Hills Drive *by J. Cole*.)*

ACUERA. That's a good thing, right?

KANSA. That's a great thing. You're them for me too.

(**ACUERA** *and* **KANSA** *make out.)*

---

*A license to produce *It's Gonna Rain* does not include a performance license for "Intro" by J. Cole. The publisher and author suggest that the licensee contact ASCAP or BMI to ascertain the rights holder to acquire permission for performance of this song. If permission is unattainable, the licensee should create an original composition in a similar style. For further information, please see music use note on page 3.

Scene Ten

(Lights of various colors fade up and down on **NISHA** *alone at the spot. She looks out over the vast expanse of Indiana forest. Near the end of the music, the lights fade to black entirely.)*

Scene Eleven

*(Fade up on **CHARLIE** and **EMILY**.)*

EMILY. Look: Before you say anything about what happened, I would just like to address that: I am sorry. About how I reacted to your... I reacted the wrong way. I should have—

CHARLIE. It's fine. Don't worry about it.

EMILY. Well, still.

CHARLIE. Thank you.

EMILY. Okay.

CHARLIE. And thanks for agreeing to come here.

EMILY. It's fine.

CHARLIE. So basically what I have to say is like—I'm sorry, just, all across the board. And... I shouldn't have done that, and I accept responsibility, and I still feel the same way about you.

EMILY. And you shouldn't have lied about it.

CHARLIE. Yeah.

(Pause.)

And it won't happen again.

EMILY. Charlie, I...

CHARLIE. Like, Seriously.

EMILY. I... I'm glad you said that. I don't know if I'm prepared to forgive you.

CHARLIE. Well...okay. Um. Do you think you might eventually?

EMILY. Eventually, yeah, I guess I probly would.

CHARLIE. So...is it okay if we like, I dunno...attempt some kind of...?

EMILY. Well, I guess we can—we can go on some dates. It's fine if we spend some time together.

CHARLIE. I'd like that.

EMILY. Okay.

Scene Twelve

(**KANSA** *and* **ACUERA** *at the spot.*)

KANSA. His mind is made up.

ACUERA. What?

KANSA. My father. He already decided, we're not…staying here, he wants to live up North at Azalea.

ACUERA. What?

KANSA. I know, (I can't)

ACUERA. You're going away?

KANSA. That is—yes.

ACUERA. Oh, so…

KANSA. I'm sorry.

ACUERA. Why are you telling me *now?*

KANSA. I didn't know until just today. I'm sorry.

ACUERA. I wouldn't have committed to Balda if I didn't think that I could be with you.

KANSA. Well—

ACUERA. I *committed,* there's no turning back. I'm nailed into this.

KANSA. I know that.

ACUERA. And, now, what!? I'm STUCK here with fucking this…working for Balda, weaving shit without a reason? And you'll be gone…

KANSA. I can't—

ACUERA. This is… I mean, what, we're breaking up?

KANSA. Quit blaming me.

ACUERA. Yeah, okay, I shouldn't blame you.

KANSA. You think this is what I *want* (or something?)

ACUERA. Well, *fuck* him, you don't (have to go)

KANSA. Yeah, Acuera, whatever, fuck him, I still have to go

ACUERA. You can't stay?

KANSA. I—

ACUERA. Stay here!

KANSA. We can't survive on our own, (Acuera.)

ACUERA. Of course we can

KANSA. We don't have a *house.*

ACUERA. We'll fucking build one!

KANSA. No…

ACUERA. *(The inaugural utterance)* I…*love* you, (and)

KANSA. Okay—

ACUERA. God, no, no I (don't)

KANSA. Will you stop being so dramatic?

ACUERA. Will you stop being so…*fallatic*!?

KANSA. What?

ACUERA. I don't know.

KANSA. I do not *want* to move away, it is not my *choice.*

ACUERA. What'll you *do* there? Can't you ask him to—

KANSA. You think I haven't?

> *(Pause.)*

You think I haven't?

ACUERA. I think you…mightn't have.

KANSA. Why would you think that?

ACUERA. It is not incontrovertibly clear that you will go to great lengths to preserve this relationship.

KANSA. Oh, you're so right. The clarity needs to be more incontrovertible.

ACUERA. Why are you hurting me?

KANSA. Acuera: *I* am not hurting you. This is not *my* fault.

ACUERA. You're right. God, you're right, why am I… blaming you, I shouldn't be… I don't know, I shouldn't be…*this*ing. Doing this.

KANSA. I *care* about you, so—

ACUERA. Yes, I know that. We need to… I don't know, we need to…is this like, our *last* time together? Is it?

KANSA. …yeah

ACUERA. God damn it, god FUCKING (DAMN IT)

KANSA. Calm (down!)

ACUERA. Fuck—FUCK THIS—

> (*KANSA interrupts ACUERA by kissing her.*)

I—

> (*They kiss again.*)

Do you feel the same way about me as I feel about you?

KANSA. Yes.

> (*They kiss and start taking off each other's clothes.*)

Scene Thirteen

>*(EMILY and NISHA are smoking a joint at the spot.)*

EMILY. It's like… I know he's a dick, but…

NISHA. I know what you mean

EMILY. I don't really know what to do anymore, but whatever. I'll just go with the flow.

NISHA. Can I say something though?

EMILY. What?

NISHA. Don't, like—don't forget that you are, in fact, fuckin awesome. So, you don't have to… You know what I'm sayin?

EMILY. Yeah. Can I say something now?

NISHA. Of course.

EMILY. Can I just say that…you did a fucking awful job rolling this?

NISHA. Can I just say that I hope you die from a bullet fired by a child soldier in Botswana?

>*(They laugh.)*

Just kidding; child soldiers aren't really an issue in Botswana.

That's actually a really serious topic.

EMILY. *(Laughs.)* I miss you.

NISHA. I'm right here.

EMILY. I know, I just…once I started dating Charlie, and you dated Mira, we kinda… I dunno, I just miss you.

NISHA. *(Mocking with faux sentimentality.)* Awwwww… dumbass…

EMILY. DUDE

NISHA. jk, I miss you.

>*(Pause.)*

I miss…the past.

(Pause.)

EMILY. She misses you too.

Scene Fourteen

(**CHARLIE** and **EMILY** replace them. They are smoking a bowl. **EMILY** lies across **CHARLIE**'s lap as he rests his hand on her breast, because that's the kind of guy he is.)

CHARLIE. Do you wanna go to Holiday World or something?

EMILY. When?

CHARLIE. Any time, just, before IU starts.

EMILY. Last time I went to Holiday World I was like 8 and I got scared going on the Liberty Launch.

CHARLIE. Well we don't have to do the Liberty Launch.

EMILY. Okay, cool.

(Pause.)

CHARLIE. We don't have to.

EMILY. No it would be fun.

(**EMILY** kisses **CHARLIE** to get his hand off her tit. They take hits.)

Thanks for coming out here with me.

CHARLIE. Yeah me too.

(Pause.)

EMILY. What?

CHARLIE. Oh, no—I just mean I'm glad we're out here.

EMILY. It's really nice out. The sky...it's like the sky has subsumed all the pink and gold in the universe. It's like the sky is made of a million oceans.

CHARLIE. Yeah.

(Pause.)

Wait, what?

EMILY. (Laughs.) Are we high?

CHARLIE. Yeah I'm pretty solid. You?

EMILY. (Suppressing laughter and using a typically unused part of the throat.) wawawa(wawawawawawawawawawawawa

CHARLIE. *(Being a cat/bird while falling into* **EMILY**'*s embrace.)* maaaaaaaaaaaawwww…maaaaaaawwwww… maaaaaawww

Scene Fifteen

(**NISHA** *and* **MIRA** *replace* **CHARLIE** *and* **EMILY**.)

NISHA. Thanks for meeting me here.

MIRA. No, I wanted to.

NISHA. So… Happy Thanksgiving I guess.

MIRA. *(Tiny laugh.)* Thanks, you too.

NISHA. How long are you here for?

MIRA. Til Saturday.

NISHA. Oh cool. Have you been…enjoying yourself?

MIRA. Yeah.

I miss home a lot though.

NISHA. I'm sorry.

MIRA. No—it's not your fault.

NISHA. Well, I know, but I'm still sorry.

MIRA. Okay.

NISHA. See, that's why I think there should be a word for
that, when you sympathize yet recognize that you had
no part in causing the misfortune.

MIRA. Yeah, I remember you think that.

NISHA. It's undeniable.

MIRA. How have you been though?

NISHA. I've been good. Except for I haven't seen you in six
million years, and I…think of you sometimes—usually
whenever it rains.

MIRA. I—

NISHA. I'm sorry, I shouldn't have said that—

MIRA. No, it's fine. I do miss you.

NISHA. Well okay. I'm sorry about that.

MIRA. Uh, I don't think you need to be sorry about that.

NISHA. Well I'm sorry that I was sorry.

(*Pause.*)

MIRA. Okay.

(Pause.)

NISHA. But I'll be fine. I guess my rational mind tells me that I'll find someone, sometime, who I feel about, like, the way I feel about—felt about you. Although at the same time, that just seems completely fucking impossible.

But all that stuff was…real, right? I didn't imagine us?

MIRA. I can't…

NISHA. Do you remember when we stopped at that random spot off the road to here, and found that bridge, and hiked up to the top of that little mountain, and there was that old hunting tower? And I made you climb with me all the way to the top, and it was creaky and shaky and we felt like we would die if the wind blew just a little bit harder? And we got to the highest platform and laid down and snuggled up under my coat, and we just stayed there in the freezing cold for hours and talked, until it was pitch black and we had no chance of getting back to the car. But we just looked at the stars and tried to stay warm in that fucking wind. And then the rain just poured on us and we got drenched. We were above the trees and on top of a tower and on top of a mountain in the rain.

We could see for miles up there. And we watched the sun setting over the frozen lake, and the birds were flying *below* us. We were higher up than any other human being on the planet and *nobody* knew we were there.

Do you remember that night?

*(After a pause, **MIRA** shakes her head "no" even though she remembers it.)*

You don't have to stay out here if you don't want to.

MIRA. It's probably best that I go.

*(**NISHA** and **MIRA** sit in silence. Slowly fade to soft and meager amber light. **MIRA** rises and walks away. **ACUERA** enters and sits downstage.*

ACUERA and NISHA are not aware of each other. Thunder rumbles. Stillness. Suddenly, we go to blackout and hear "It's Gonna Rain, Part I," from the 1965 Steve Reich piece.)*

End of Play

---

*A license to produce *It's Gonna Rain* does not include a performance license for "It's Gonna Rain, Part I," by Steve Reich. The publisher and author suggest that the licensee contact ASCAP or BMI to ascertain the rights holder to acquire permission for performance of this song. If permission is unattainable, the licensee should create an original composition in a similar style. For further information, please see music use note on page 3.